### *"How's*

"Fine," Jo replied.

"What did you name him?"

"I didn't. I told you, I don't keep strays. He's just temporary."

"Sure, sure, but he should still have a name."

Jo had a sudden inspiration born of some complex mixture of annoyance and fascination. "Let's see . . . he's already scratched me once, gotten fur all over my favorite sweater and hogged all the tuna fish. I think I'll name him after you."

She had the satisfaction of having surprised him, but then he bounced right back. "I'm honored." His voice dropped slightly as his eyes held hers. "Not to mention a little envious."

It was her turn to be surprised. "Why?"

He stood up. "Because I'd be willing to bet that Wilson slept with you last night."

Dear Reader,

When two people fall in love, the world is suddenly new and exciting, and it's that same excitement we bring to you in Silhouette Intimate Moments. These are stories with scope, with grandeur. The characters lead the lives we all dream of, and everything they do reflects the wonder of being in love.

Longer and more sensuous than most romances, Silhouette Intimate Moments novels take you away from everyday life and let you share the magic of love. Adventure, glamour, drama, even suspense— these are the passwords that let you into a world where love has a power beyond the ordinary, where the best authors in the field today create stories of love and commitment that will stay with you always.

In coming months look for novels by your favorite authors: Maura Seger, Parris Afton Bonds, Linda Howard and Nora Roberts, to name just a few. And whenever you buy books, look for all the Silhouette Intimate Moments, love stories *for* today's women *by* today's women.

Leslie J. Wainger
Senior Editor
Silhouette Books

# Maura Seger

# Conflict of Interest

Silhouette Intimate Moments

Published by Silhouette Books New York

**America's Publisher of Contemporary Romance**

SILHOUETTE BOOKS
300 East 42nd St., New York, N.Y. 10017

Copyright © 1988 by Maura Seger

All rights reserved, including the right to reproduce
this book or portions thereof in any form whatsoever.
For information address Silhouette Books,
300 East 42nd St., New York, N.Y. 10017

ISBN: 0-373-07236-8

First Silhouette Books printing April 1988

All the characters in this book are fictitious. Any
resemblance to actual persons, living or dead, is
purely coincidental.

SILHOUETTE, SILHOUETTE INTIMATE MOMENTS and colophon
are registered trademarks of the publisher.

America's Publisher of Contemporary Romance

Printed in the U.S.A.

## *MAURA SEGER*

was prompted by a love of books and a vivid imagination to decide, at age twelve, to be a writer. Twenty years later her first book was published. So much, she says, for overnight success! Now each book is an adventure, filled with fascinating people who always surprise her.

# Chapter 1

Just one of *those* days. Whoever had coined that phrase had, in Jo Blakely's opinion, understated the case. Days like the one she was having should be outlawed on the simple grounds of humanitarianism. Surely they were covered somewhere under the articles of the Geneva convention? If not, she would lead the movement to have them amended.

She had awakened to discover that a power failure had disabled her alarm clock. Stumbling from bed, it dawned on her that meant there would be no water, hence no coffee and no shower. That was almost enough to drive her back under the covers, especially when a glance out the window of her Georgetown apartment revealed that while there might not be water inside, there was plenty outside. It was raining like the proverbial cats and dogs—big, fat, arrogant drops just waiting to turn her chestnut-brown hair lank, blur her mascara and trickle down the back of her neck to undoubtedly give her a cold.

She stared glumly at herself in the bathroom mirror as she tried, with something less than success, to throw off the effects of sleep. Lacking the accustomed jolt of caffeine—which she resolved every New Year's to give up—her body was less than cooperative. Not to mention her mind, which felt as leaden as the sky she had glimpsed beyond her windows.

Nonetheless she persevered as far as the lack of electricity would permit. A bottle of mineral water fresh from the refrigerator provided a brisk, invigorating face wash. When she looked at herself in the mirror again, her fair skin glowed. Her face, triangular in shape, was set with wide gray eyes, a straight nose she privately thought a shade too short and a full mouth that smiled readily. She had a firm chin, which those who believed in such things claimed indicated stubbornness, and in her case, they were right.

As a child, she had attended ballet classes after school even though it had meant her mother had to drive her twenty miles each way to the nearest town. Alicia Blakely had done so because she said her daughter needed a feminine touch in her life that would not be easily found on the ranch where they lived. Jo had started out hating the lessons that made her feel different from her friends, but she had ended by loving them. There had even been times when she had dreamed of a career as a ballerina. She could still remember that dream fondly, even though she had long since moved on to other things.

Not the least of those other things was her job, which she really had to get to quickly. The day had begun inauspiciously, and it hardly surprised her to discover that her last pair of panty hose had apparently been packaged with a run in them. The dry cleaner had torn the hem of the black pleated skirt she had intended to wear, and the beige silk blouse she tried to put on was missing a button. She sneezed glumly and reached for a tissue, only to find herself fumbling with an empty box.

"Drat," she muttered as she tossed the box away and went back to burrowing in her closet for something else to wear. Not for the first time in her twenty-eight years, she regretted the lack of a more explicit vocabulary.

She finally emerged clutching a pair of dark blue linen slacks and a mauve angora turtleneck. She dragged them on, consoling herself that while the slacks were a little snug, they at least had the virtue of hiding the run in her stockings. They also had a matching jacket which gave the ensemble a business-like air.

After stabbing herself twice with her pierced earrings, she finally managed to get them on, but gave up on the gold bracelet with the recalcitrant catch. She slid her feet into a pair of black pumps, took the left one off to extract a paper clip that had somehow found its way to the toe and eventually managed to get herself out to the hall closet where—miraculously—her raincoat and umbrella were waiting for her.

With her pocketbook and briefcase in one hand and the umbrella in the other, she ran down the steps of the town house and emerged onto the street in time to see her bus whizzing by. Grimly gripping the umbrella to prevent it from blowing away in the gusting wind, she trudged to the bus stop to wait.

As she did, a large black limousine went by, driving straight through a muddy puddle, splashing most of the contents onto Jo's raincoat. She alternated between dabbing at them ineffectively and glaring at the offending vehicle as it disappeared around the corner without pausing.

"Of all the..." Two years in Washington, D.C., had resigned her to a certain level of rudeness, but they still had not accustomed her to quite the degree of unconcern people could—and did—show for each other. Part of her still wanted to believe that most of her fellow Washingtonians were really just like the folks back home in Oklahoma.

Another part of her had learned better, yet the idealism that had first drawn her to the nation's capital and to a career in politics lingered. She believed that individuals could make a difference, and she was determined to be one of those who did.

Since coming to Washington four years before, she had been fortunate enough to be able to live in the exclusive Georgetown neighborhood, which managed, despite its closeness to the sprawling city, to preserve much of the atmosphere of an earlier time. There was a graciousness about the place that made it extremely desirable to both long-term Washington residents and new arrivals. Narrow streets, brick sidewalks and elegant Federal-style town houses made Georgetown a distinct and very special community.

Jo felt privileged to be able to live there, particularly since the rent she paid was modest in comparison to what her apartment could have commanded.

Her landlord had been less interested in making a profit than in acquiring a congenial tenant. A mutual acquaintance had introduced them at a time when Jo was beginning to despair of finding a place to live that didn't involve an hour or more of commuting. Since she tended to work late, often well into the evening, she had visions of having to sleep in the office, until fate had intervened in the form of the perfect apartment.

When the second bus came along, she crammed into it along with the dozen or so other people who had been waiting. After enduring the jolting ride downtown, which took almost twice as long as usual, she emerged at the stop nearest the Capitol Building with a definite sense of relief. Surely the day had to get better.

The side entrance she usually used because of its convenience to the office wing was some distance away from where the bus stopped. Rather than tramp through the rain, Jo scrambled up the wide stone steps to the main entrance. There were usually tourists perched there, staring at their guidebooks or simply looking around, taking stock. But this morning the steps were deserted, thanks to the weather.

She paused at the huge bronze doors that led to the Rotunda and shook out her umbrella. Her footsteps echoed as she crossed the marble floor inside. She glanced in passing at the massive oil paintings that depicted the story of the nation's founding. When Jo had first come to Washington, she had found excuses to use this entrance to the Capitol, unashamed to be stirred by the reminders of her country's history. But after a while, the novelty had worn off, and she became too absorbed in her work to think of much else. As she walked through the Rotunda, Jo decided that she ought to pick her head up a little more often and take note of where she was. It never hurt to remember.

The miniature subway, which connected the Capitol with the Senate and House office buildings on either side, was crowded despite the relatively early hour. As Jo squeezed onto it, one of her co-workers spotted her and waved.

Shelley Henderson was a hardheaded blonde on the far side of forty who had worked in Washington almost twenty years and firmly believed that things were never so bad that they couldn't get worse. Experience had long since proven her right, but Jo still refused to believe it.

"There's nothing serious on the agenda today, for a change," Shelley said as they left the subway, walked up the stairs to the second floor and entered the offices where they worked. The spacious, high-ceilinged area was furnished with several masculine-looking leather couches, half a dozen oak desks for the lower-level assistants and the usual word processing and telephone equipment. Beyond were two small offices belonging to Jo and Shelley. Adjacent to them was a closed door that shielded what they all half jokingly referred to as "the inner sanctum."

"He's already in," Shelley said, glancing toward the door. "Doesn't the man ever go home?"

"Of course he does," Jo said as she stripped off her sodden coat and hung it on the rack to dry. "Don't you read your own handouts? He's a devoted family man."

"Actually, he is," Shelley said as she instinctively homed in on the coffee machine. As she poured herself a mugful, she shook her head. "Besides, how many United States senators make coffee? Most of them would rather chop off their fingers than do that."

Jo poured a cup for herself and took a sip, all but closing her eyes with relief as the first jolt of caffeine spread through her. When she wasn't thinking of giving up coffee altogether, she resolved to at least switch to the decaffeinated variety, just as she kept meaning to lose ten pounds and find a really good hairdresser. It was good to have goals in life, no matter how unrealistic.

"Greeley's different. He's got too much integrity to care about the trappings of his rank. People sense that about him. That's one of the reasons they like him as much as they do."

"Liking is one thing," Shelley said. "Voting for him is another. The voters have been burned too often. They have to really believe he can do the job, or they won't go for him."

"They'll believe it," Jo said with conviction. "Or at least they will by the time we get to the convention. All the polls show he's gaining."

Shelley shrugged and headed for her cubicle. "Polls don't make a president; only votes do that. I'll feel a whole lot better when this election is history."

One of the six phone lines coming into the senator's office rang. Jo went to her desk to answer it. Moments later she was immersed in the minutiae of her job, trying to sort out a problem for a constituent who was convinced that if he couldn't reach the senator himself, only his top assistant would do. Jo listened patiently and assured him she would take care of the matter, before she was finally able to get off the phone. Barely had she done so than the red light on her desk blinked twice. The senator wanted to see her.

He was seated at the large mahogany desk which was said to have once belonged to Admiral John Paul Jones and had been in the Greeley family for several generations. Jason Greeley's mother had sent it to Washington when her son won his first election.

It was, as always, covered with a sea of papers organized according to some mysterious system only the senator himself could understand. Staff members jokingly said that he would never need a shredder since no one else would ever be able to discover his secrets. Given the political scandals that had plagued certain recent administrations, the joke was just a bit nervous.

"Sit down," Jason said when she appeared at the door. "Great weather, isn't it?"

She smiled and walked across the room to take a seat on the other side of the desk. As she did so, she observed him, noticing that despite the thinning hair that was already in disarray, the slightly undone tie and the rolled-up shirtsleeves, he managed to retain the air of grace under pressure that was his trademark. It did not escape her, however, that there were shadows beneath his blue eyes. If he hadn't been up all night, he had come pretty close to it.

"Let me check with the farmers before I comment," she said banteringly. "They might feel we need the rain."

"I hope somebody does," he muttered and put a hand up to stifle a yawn.

"Rough night?" Jo asked.

Jason nodded. A less knowledgeable listener might have expected him to make some comment about agonizing over vital national issues, but Jo wasn't at all surprised when he said, "Hilary's down again with that throat infection she keeps getting. Marianne had been up with her two nights running, so I was trying to give her a break."

Marianne was the senator's wife, a petite, soft-voiced woman whom he had married against the wishes of his family when they were both freshmen at the University of North Carolina. They had four children ranging in age from twenty to three, Hilary being the youngest. The senator affectionately referred to her as his little surprise since she had come along after they had thought their family was complete.

"I hope she'll be all right," Jo said gently. "What does the doctor say?"

"That she'll grow out of it and until she does, we have to live with it. He doesn't hold with yanking tonsils out."

"I'm sure he's right, but it must be awfully hard to see her go through that."

"She's a trooper, though. Never complains, never asks for any sympathy. Although," he added with a smile, "she did mention something about the best cure being a steady diet of ice cream."

"She wouldn't, by any chance, be picking up her father's talent for politics, would she?"

"Lord, I hope not. That's the last thing I'd want her to get into."

Jo frowned. It wasn't like the senator to sound so down; his was normally the steadiest of natures. Even when exhausted, as he frequently was these days, he still tended to see the bright side of any situation.

Gently she asked, "Want to tell me what's wrong?"

He ran a hand through his silvery hair and gave her an apologetic smile. "Nothing really, it's just that this whole business is starting to get to me a little."

She didn't have to ask what he meant by that. The campaign on which the senator had embarked the previous year had been long and hard, and it was by no means over yet. On the contrary, his early successes and his front-runner status in the polls had simply made the pressure on him all the more intense. So far he seemed to be dealing with it very well, but Jo wasn't surprised that his patience was wearing thin.

Still, she was mindful that they had a long way to go yet and could only hope that he would be able to hold on. It was commonplace wisdom around Washington that anyone who survived a presidential campaign found the presidency itself relatively restful. Jo didn't quite go that far in her own thinking, but she understood the point.

There were times when she thought that the campaign's ultimate effect was to dissuade people from seeking the office rather than to assist voters in making the best selection. Certainly neither the public nor their elected officials were served by it.

Every few years people were reminded of how cumbersome and tedious a process it had become. Inevitably there was talk of reform, but nothing much ever seemed to come of it.

"I found this waiting for me this morning," Jason said, sliding a piece of paper across the desk to her.

She took it and scanned the neatly typed sentences. Immediately her eyebrows rose. "David Wilson?"

The senator nodded. "Having the courtesy to inform me that he's going to be covering my campaign." He gestured toward the letter. "In-depth, as he says. We can expect him anytime."

"Does Shelley know about this?"

He shook his head. "Not yet. I'll tell her after we've talked. Naturally she'll be worried. Wilson's reputation as a gunslinger is well earned."

"Shelley can handle him. She's one of the best public relations people in the business." Greeley, kind though he could be, did not tolerate slouches on his payroll. Shelley's principal task was to keep him in close contact with his constituents back home, and she did that job extremely well.

"I agree," the senator said, "but I wouldn't normally turn this over to her anyway. I'd give it to somebody on the campaign staff. The only problem is that I've got the feeling that's the wrong tack to take with Wilson. He goes through media types like a hot knife through butter."

"Maybe, but I'd be willing to bet on Shelley stopping him. She's tough."

Jason nodded. "As nails, but if somehow she was able to run interference with Wilson, that would only get his back up. Under those circumstances, there's nothing to stop him from coming down on us with everything he's got."

Jo pondered for a moment, then nodded slowly. "What you seem to be saying is that if he gets any idea we're trying to snow him, he'll tear us apart."

"That's about the size of it," the senator agreed. "Besides, there's another consideration. Shelley's on the payroll for the office staff, not the campaign. That's more than a formality. The two sides are supposed to be kept distinct."

"You know it doesn't always work out that way," she reminded him quietly. "Other candidates aren't necessarily so scrupulous."

Jason shrugged. "That doesn't make any difference to me. If I based my behavior on what other people do, I wouldn't have insisted on splitting your salary between this office and the campaign when you started helping out on speeches."

"True," Jo agreed. "But to get back to the problem, somebody has to deal with Wilson."

"Exactly." He leaned back in his leather desk-chair and smiled at her.

"Oh, no," Jo exclaimed, "not me. I'm up to my ears as it is. The last thing I need is a David Wilson tossed into my lap."

The senator waved a hand in dismissal. "You can handle it. You're the best administrative assistant on the Hill, and you're turning out to be damn helpful in the campaign, too. Wilson couldn't complain that he was getting shorted on either side. You know one of the issues he's going to be looking at is whether or not my constituents have been shortchanged by my being out on the hustings. You're in the best possible position to answer that."

"Thanks," Jo murmured. "I'll remind you of how indispensable and versatile I am the next time I'm up for a raise. But as for the rest, no, I can't. I'd be absolutely no good at this at all. In fact, I'd be a disaster. Take my word for it."

The senator shook his head. He gave her his best, his most sincere look—the same one that smiled out of his campaign posters. "I have complete faith in your ability to handle this; otherwise I wouldn't be assigning it to you."

Jo opened her mouth to protest further, only to close it with a snap. Jason Greeley was a very nice man, never pushy or dictatorial, always considerate and respectful of other people. But when he arrived at a decision about something, nothing on heaven or earth could move him. She could talk herself blue in the face, and he wouldn't change his mind.

"I'll see what I can find on Wilson," she muttered as she stood up.

"Good." As she turned to go, he called after her softly, "Jo, I meant what I said. You really can handle this."

She managed a faint smile over her shoulder. "At least I'll give it my best shot. You can count on that."

Several hours later, as she pored over the material she had managed to assemble on David Wilson, she wondered whether her best was going to be anywhere good enough. However she looked at it, he was bad news. A network commentator with a reputation for tough, insightful analysis, he took particular delight in exposing phonies and liars.

That the senator was not either of those things didn't reassure her. Plenty of perfectly well-meaning people had been shown up as inadequate on television under Wilson's unrelenting stare. He was a master of the catchy phrase, the memorable line that, once attached to a public figure, tended to follow him forever.

Above all, he seemed to be intensely suspicious of anyone who aspired to great power. Would-be presidents were his speciality. He had shredded so many he must have lost count.

All of that was well and good, but Jo was absolutely determined that Jason Greeley wasn't going to be next on Wilson's hit list. She would do her best to cooperate with the newsman so that he could get a fair, accurate picture of the senator. But at the first hint of a smear campaign, she was going to cry foul.

Her chin was firmly set as she closed the folder and rubbed the back of her neck beneath her short, curly hair. Her full mouth was drawn into a resolute line, and her gray eyes blazed. If her brothers had been able to see her then, they would have recognized that she had her dander up.

The tall man who stood watching her from the cubicle entrance had much the same impression.

He was several inches over six feet, with the slim, rangy body of a runner or a tennis player. His dark blond hair was slightly longer than current style dictated. His face was square shaped and rugged with assertive features. His deep-set, compelling brown eyes stared out at the world with energy and intelligence. He was dressed casually in twill slacks, a blue cotton shirt and a tweed jacket. Rain had splattered his broad shoulders and dampened his hair.

He made no sound nor did he move, but only scant seconds passed before Jo became aware of his presence. She looked up, feeling his gaze on her, and her eyes widened. Not, she assured herself quickly, because he was so good-looking.

In point of fact, his features were a bit too tough for her taste. He looked like a man who had been through hard times and hadn't forgotten any of them. But on television the impact of his presence was diluted, at least a little. Faced with the full force of his considerable personality, she had to take a deep breath to steady herself.

"Won't you come in and sit down, Mr. Wilson," she said as she rose. She surreptitiously wiped her damp palms on the legs of her slacks and indicated the chair across from her desk.

"Thanks." He dropped into the chair, stretched out his long legs and continued to stare at her. After a moment, Jo reluctantly resumed her own seat. Reluctantly, because she would have much preferred to leave right then and there.

Instead she said, "We've been expecting you."

He raised his eyebrows mockingly. "With bated breath, I suppose. Where's Greeley?"

His abrupt, sarcastic manner didn't sit well with Jo, even though she realized that it was a technique he had honed through long experience. She couldn't help but frown as she said, "On the Senate floor. An important vote is coming up on highway appropriations."

"And he doesn't want to miss the chance to grease a few palms back home, not to mention helping to put some money in the pockets of other politicos he hopes will support him."

Temper, temper, Jo murmured to herself. He was only trying to provoke her into an unguarded response, which was absolutely the last thing she was willing to give him. Instead she merely smiled. "If you say so, Mr. Wilson."

She leaned her arms on her desk, her hands folded, the picture of competence and confidence. "Now then, suppose we talk about how I can assist you. When did you plan to start interviewing the senator?"

David leaned back in his chair, his long legs stretched out in front of him. He was as close as he could get to slouching without actually doing it. His posture not only proclaimed him to be completely relaxed but also suggested that he didn't attach any great importance to the situation. It was as though he hadn't quite decided yet whether or not Greeley—and the people who worked for him—needed to be taken seriously.

"I don't," he said. "At least not for a while. He's got his answers down pat to just about any question I could come up with at this point. I want to watch him first, get some idea of how he ticks before we sit down for a chat."

Jo had never encountered that kind of approach before. None of the network correspondents she knew was particularly big on getting background. They tended to breeze in, do a superficial interview and breeze out again.

What they claimed were the unavoidable demands of their medium led candidates to speak, and even think, in fifteen-second bursts that could be easily dropped into the nightly news. This process made a mockery of the vital issues of the day, but there didn't seem to be anything that could be done about it.

Objectively she had to admit that David's approach made a lot more sense, even if it was harder for everyone concerned. But he had annoyed her enough that she wasn't about to tell him that.

"Nonetheless," she said with a frosty smile, "it's reassuring to know that you do eventually intend to speak with the senator. I'm sure it would be much more convenient for you if you could simply give your opinions about him without being troubled by anything as cumbersome as facts."

David bared his teeth in what no one over the age of three would have taken for a smile. "Hit a nerve, did I? Good. I find that I get the best results when people are just a wee bit nervous around me. They tend to reveal more than they realize."

"Such as?"

He paused a moment, looked at her steadily and said, "Such as the fact that you're devoted to the senator to the extent that you feel you have to be protective of him. There may be a little hero worship involved, maybe something more. He's an attractive man, and there's a possibility that you could think of him in other than strictly businesslike terms."

He paused to see if she would rise to the bait. When she refused to do so, he went on. "You've got a very slight Oklahoma accent, so being here in Washington, personal assistant to a man of his stature, must be a very big deal to you. You aren't married, and my guess is you aren't dating anyone seriously. You left the house in a hurry this morning, and you've had an extremely busy day including lunch at your desk. That isn't good for your digestion, so how about having dinner with me?''

Jo sat and stared at him. She knew she had to say something, but she had no idea where to begin. Finally she took a deep breath and dived in headfirst.

"You're out of line with your speculation about the senator and me. If you insist on pursuing the possibility of any unprofessional involvement between us, you'll come up dry, but feel free to waste your time if you like. Yes, I'm from Oklahoma originally, but I've been in the big city a long time, so if you think you're dealing with a dumb little country girl, you're in for a nasty surprise. I'm not wearing a wedding ring, so it hardly takes a genius to figure out I'm not married. However, I would like to know how you came up with the rest.''

"Simple," he said with a look that suggested he thought it actually was. "You look sufficiently like the romantic type so that if there was a serious boyfriend around, you'd have a picture of him somewhere in evidence. Probably in a silver frame and probably taken during some special event you look back on fondly. You left the house in a hurry because you put your wristwatch on upside down.''

Jo glanced at it, surprised to discover that he was correct. "How on earth . . .''

"Beats me. That's pretty tough to do. You wouldn't be ambidextrous, would you?" When she shook her head, he shrugged. "Anyway, you had lunch at your desk because the remnants are in the trash. Dinner because you're the best-looking woman I've seen in a while, and I could do with some company.''

"I buy it right up to the end," Jo told him. "The best-looking part doesn't fly. Considering the circles you move in, that couldn't possibly be true. As for the needing company angle, it would work better with violins in the background. I'm really supposed to believe that the great and illustrious David Wilson is lonely and stuck for a date?"

"Hey," he said, raising his hands palms up. "I didn't go that far. But what's wrong with wanting to get acquainted?"

"Nothing, provided you're up-front about the reason. You're covering Greeley. Given your style of reporting, that means you're covering everyone involved with him. So any conversation we have is on the record and strictly business. Agreed?"

He grinned at her sheepishly. "You drive a hard bargain."

She closed the file she'd been studying, glad that he hadn't noticed it was on him, and walked around the corner of the desk. "You're right again, Mr. Wilson."

He rose and stood aside to let her pass, then followed her into the outer office. As she went to put on her raincoat, he took it from her and held it while she slipped her arms into the sleeves. He opened the door for her, and they went out. "How about making it David?" he asked as they walked down the marble corridor to the elevators.

"All right, but it won't make any difference. You and I aren't going to be friends."

"Want to bet?" he murmured under his breath.

"What was that?"

"Never mind. Whatever you say, Ms. Blakely—Jo. You're calling the shots."

She gave him a dubious look, wondering exactly what she was getting into and how fast she could find a way out.

## Chapter 2

Trying to get a taxi at that hour would have been futile, but Jo was still surprised when, after leaving the Capitol, they strolled down the mall in the direction of the Washington Monument.

It was still drizzling, but off toward the west, patches of clear sky could be seen. While official Washington was winding down its day, the tourists were still out in force. The cherry trees were trying to come into bloom, and, as though to encourage them, cameras were clicking away.

"Did you have any particular place in mind?" Jo asked when they left the mall and turned north toward Constitution Avenue. They were nearing the White House and the select cluster of restaurants that served its elite staff. The limousines were thick in this part of town. Jo stepped carefully to avoid getting splashed again.

"I thought we'd give that new place, Maison Georgette, a try," David said.

Jo's eyebrows rose. With a sardonic smile, she said, "It sounds as though I'm about to get an object lesson in the power of the media."

"How's that?"

"You know perfectly well that it's useless to try to get into Maison Georgette without a reservation, unless you happen to be at the top of the heap in this town. Getting past Edouard—" she referred to the restaurant's formidable maître d' "—is an exercise in muscle flexing."

"So you think I'm trying to impress you?" David asked with a grin.

"Impress or scare. Either way, I assure you it isn't necessary."

He stopped walking, looked at her and said, "That's a relief. My expense account could use a rest. How about a hamburger instead?"

At her wrinkled nose, he laughed. "Do I gather you'd rather be impressed?"

She shrugged without apology as they resumed walking. "When it comes right down to it, I'm as susceptible to the good life as the next person."

He shot her a single penetrating look from his dark brown eyes. "I doubt that."

"Why?" she asked as they stepped inside Maison Georgette. The entry hall was small and crowded with elegantly dressed men and women waiting for a place at the bar, where they would then wait for a table. For the lucky few with clout, Edouard was on hand to escort them directly into the inner sanctum.

Edouard was a tall, ascetic-looking man with refined features and an intimidating manner. In a single all-encompassing glance he could instantly gauge the quality of one's dress, the level of one's status and the degree, if any, of one's leverage in a town where that was worth more than gold.

Jo couldn't help but notice that every man and most of the women within her view were meticulously outfitted in the de rigueur dark business suit that shrieked of shockingly expensive tailoring. Only David was more casually dressed and apparently completely unconcerned about his attire.

Edouard glanced in their direction and, wonder of wonders, his pale narrow face broke into a broad smile. "Ah, Mr. Wilson, how nice. And..." He paused for barely a split second as the computer he had for a mind put a name to Jo's face. "Miss Blakely. How delightful that you could both join us this evening. A quiet table, I presume?"

"Absolutely," David told him with a grin. "Ms. Blakely and I have a great deal to talk about."

Edouard nodded complacently as he escorted them inside. "Of course, but you must dine as well. Too much talk on an empty stomach leads to disagreements."

"We wouldn't want that, would we?" David asked as he remained standing while Jo was seated. His unexpected courtesy startled her. Living in what was still essentially a man's town, she was more accustomed to the niceties being ignored.

Edouard snapped his fingers and instantly two waiters appeared beside them. "I will leave you in good hands," he said. "But if I can be of further assistance..." He left the sentence uncompleted, conveying the impression that there were no limits to the service he would be only too happy to provide.

"I can see why this place has become so popular," Jo murmured as she accepted a menu from one of the waiters and glanced around.

Off to her left, she recognized the President's chief of staff in conversation with a high-ranking member of the Justice department. Nearby the senior senator from a major southern state was dining with two men Jo knew as lobbyists for the oil industry. The senator glanced in her direction and smiled.

"If a bomb went off in here right now," David said, "a good argument could be made that the country would be a whole lot better off. Present company excepted, of course."

Jo sat back, took a quick look at the menu and asked, "Have you always been so cynical?"

David pondered that for a moment. "Yes," he said at length, "I think I was born this way. Why, does it bother you?"

"Not really. It's more your problem than mine. Obviously no one survives in Washington by being naive. But it does seem a shame to me whenever someone falls into the trap of automatically thinking everything has a price."

"Do you really believe that isn't so?"

"I *know* it isn't," she said softly. "There are plenty of honest people in Washington and all over. People who believe in what they're doing and who work hard to accomplish it."

He put his menu down and rested his arms on the table. Her gaze was drawn to his firm mouth. She watched as he said, "Now I suppose you're going to tell me that Greeley is one of them."

She shrugged and looked away. "If I do, will you believe me?"

"That depends."

"On what?"

"On whether or not the evidence supports you. So far he's come through this campaign smelling like a rose. Dedicated public servant, devoted family man, born leader, the whole ball of wax. He's for a strong America at peace with the world, industrial renewal and full employment, equal rights for all and mom's apple pie. How could anyone not vote for the guy?"

Jo bristled. She was finding David's skepticism difficult to take. "It's easy to make fun of a man who's sincere in his convictions, but can you offer anything better?"

"Yes," he said flatly. "Truth. It's a rare commodity, all right, but in the final analysis it's the best protection our country has."

"But Jason Greeley is telling the truth," Jo insisted. "His policies are exactly as he states."

David waited to answer until after the waiter had taken their drink orders. "Are you telling me," he asked, "that Greeley is being absolutely frank about everything he says? He doesn't tailor his statements to particular audiences? He never shades his views so that they seem simpler than they really are and people can remember them more easily? He never makes a quick, dramatic statement that he knows will get him on the nightly news?"

Jo flushed. Everything David mentioned struck all too close to home. No one on the Greeley campaign liked it, least of all the senator himself, but the fact remained that there were certain things which had to be done in order to wage a successful campaign. Oversimplification and the occasional shading of views were chief among them.

"There are certain realities to politics today," she ventured before David cut her off with an abrupt slash of his hand through the air.

"That's the excuse I hear all the time. The system made me do it. Everybody says that, from the kid who rips off some little old lady for her social security check to the politician who doesn't tell the public the truth because he doesn't think they're smart enough to deal with it."

"Jason doesn't think that," Jo protested. "If he didn't have so much respect and, yes, love for the American people, he wouldn't care about being president."

David sat back in his chair and looked at her with frank disbelief. "Remember those violins you mentioned a while back?"

Jo forced herself to take a deep breath. She couldn't remember the last time anyone had provoked her as much as David Wilson did. It seemed as though he had only to speak for her to get her back up. But anger wouldn't serve any purpose. If she was going to deal with him successfully, she had to stay cool, calm and collected.

The smile she gave him would have done the Mona Lisa proud. He could read nothing behind it except an absolute refusal to rise to the bait he so expertly offered.

"There's something I'm curious about," she said as the waiter set their drinks before them. "How do you balance your blatant cynicism with the responsibility of the journalist to be objective?"

"It's not easy," David said bluntly. He took a sip of his Scotch and water before continuing. "But I always keep in mind the fact that objective doesn't mean nice. I'm not paid to cozy up to the movers and shakers of this world and get them to like me. On the contrary, it's my job to ask the questions ordinary people are wondering about but never get a chance to ask for themselves. They have a right to see past the surface veneer to whatever happens to be underneath it, good or bad."

"So, in a sense, you see yourself as a champion for the man—and woman—in the street?"

He nodded a bit abashedly. "I suppose you could put it that way."

"How much do you think they care?"

For just a moment something flitted behind his eyes—surprise, concern, some combination of both. "It's hard to tell," he said slowly. "Sometimes it does seem that you have to shout awfully loud to get most people's attention."

"So you do understand about having to make concessions to whatever particular audience you're trying to reach." Before he could comment, a detail she had come across in the file on him occurred to Jo. "You used to be a writer. If I remember, you wrote several books that were bestsellers."

David nodded. "Do you know what that means, being a bestselling author?"

"That you made a lot of money?"

He laughed ruefully. Her frankness was refreshing, if a bit disconcerting. "Besides that. Those books sold a couple of million copies between them. That includes both hardcover and paperback. It's nothing to sneer at, but it's a drop in the bucket compared to the number of people television reaches."

"Is that why you changed careers?"

He gave an exaggerated wince, as though she had wounded him. "I like to think I'm still in the same line of work. After all, I do write everything I broadcast."

Jo was only too aware that many of the top television news personalities were merely figureheads who were paid enormous sums to parrot other people's words. Somewhere along the line she had heard that David operated differently, which was probably one of the reasons he was considered to have lethal potential in his reporting.

She took another look at the menu, then smiled at him. "Are you trying to tell me that you don't want to be just another pretty face?"

He was a bit taken aback at her choice of phrase, but responded quickly. "No more than you would. Nobody gets to the position you hold without having plenty on the ball. Suppose you tell me what made you decide to work for Greeley?"

"He offered me a job," Jo said succinctly, then they broke off the conversation to order.

"What's good?" David asked the waiter. If the solemn-faced gentleman was perturbed by having so blunt a question posed in what was being lauded as a temple to gastronomic excellence, he managed to hide it well. He made several suggestions, and they selected those that sounded most appealing.

When the waiter had retreated, David said, "Back to you. You were minding your business one day when out of nowhere Greeley offered you a job."

Jo grinned and shook her head. She fought a brief battle with her conscience, lost it and helped herself to a slice of warm, fattening French bread. She did, however, forgo the butter.

"Hmm, that's great, you should try some. I was finishing up at the Columbia J School." She presumed that he would understand the shorthand reference to what was one of the leading institutes of journalism in the world. "Naturally," she went on, "I was thinking a lot about what I'd do when I got out. I'd had the usual round of interviews for jobs on newspapers and a couple of TV stations. There were a few possibilities that looked promising, but I couldn't work up as much enthusiasm for them as I thought I should. Then I got to thinking about Greeley. He was running for reelection to his senate seat, and I liked what he had to say, so I wrote to him."

"A fan letter?"

"Sort of," she admitted. "I admired what he stood for, but I didn't make a big point of that. Instead I said that I was rather belatedly considering a career in public life and did he have any suggestions?"

"Let me guess, in the middle of his reelection campaign, he dropped everything to give you job counseling?"

Jo shook her head. "I got a form letter asking me to give one of his assistants a call. That turned out to be Shelley Henderson. She talked to me, then reported back to the senator. A few days later I found myself sitting down with him for all of two minutes while he explained that he'd decided to put on an extra press aide, and did I want the job.''

"What did you say?"

"Yes, of course. I went to work that afternoon. By the time the campaign was over, I figured if I could survive that, I could survive anything. So I stayed."

"How did you go from assistant press aide to being Greeley's right-hand man . . . sorry, person?"

Jo stifled a sigh. She disliked talking about herself to strangers and was getting tired of the conversation very quickly. But she supposed that she had to satisfy his curiosity before they could move on to other things.

"I have an excellent memory for details," she said frankly, "I'm able to get along with just about any kind of person, I can do twelve things at the same time and, in a pinch, I can twist arms. So, as you can see, I'm ideally suited to the job."

"Sounds like you are," he agreed, impressed despite himself. She was more than he had expected, a whole lot more. In his experience, top senatorial aides were lean and hungry young people, out to amass as much power for themselves as they possibly could and parlay their jobs into a chance to hold elected office on their own.

Failing that, they wanted to be lobbyists, which tended to pay better anyway. Few seemed dedicated to the position itself. Jo was an exception. For all that he claimed to be a cynic, he could not deny that she seemed genuine in her ideals.

"Greeley's lucky to have you," he said, somewhat grudgingly. He came very close to adding that any man would be. There was something about her—he couldn't exactly put his finger on it—that made her extremely appealing to him.

It had to do in part with her looks: she wasn't precisely beautiful, but there was an animation and intelligence about her features that drew him strongly. He also liked the fact that in a town where too many women looked like department store mannequins, Jo had curves.

On a less chauvinistic note, he had a sense of her as an open, forthright person, something he didn't encounter all that often. He was half afraid that if he got to know her better, he would end up finding out that she wasn't as he imagined. But he had already decided to take that risk.

"Thank you," she said gravely. "Now how about telling me about yourself?"

He swallowed a bite of his gray sole in puff pastry and asked, "Didn't that file you were reading fill you in?"

Jo laughed ruefully. "There isn't much you miss, is there?"

"I sure hope not. Anyway, what do you want to know?"

She looked at him for a long moment, seeing the strength and resolution in his features, the solid, masculine appeal that owed nothing to artifice. There was something very familiar about him. It took her a moment to pin it down.

"Have you spent much time out west?"

"You mean in California?"

"Not really...more like Wyoming, Montana, Oklahoma."

"Can't say that I have."

"Texas then," she persisted. "New Mexico?"

"Try again."

"South Dakota, Colorado? Do I get a prize if I can name all the states?"

He grinned at her teasingly. "Only if you remember Delaware. That's where I'm from originally."

"Delaware?"

"On the other side of the Chesapeake, half swamped by Virginia?"

"I know where it is," she told him. "I've even been there."

"What did you think of it?"

"Uh...parts were very pretty. The people were quite nice. Unfortunately I'm not that crazy about crabs and there didn't seem...."

"To be much else to the place?" he finished for her. "Actually there is, but it's true that when you think excitement, you don't necessarily think of Delaware first."

"I had you figured for the wide open spaces," she admitted. "A ranch maybe. Some place where you'd tested yourself against some harsh realities."

"Is that where you're from?"

She nodded. "In Oklahoma my folks have a place near Chickasha."

"Not *the* Chickasha?"

"Okay, so it isn't the hub of the world, but it's a nice place."

"Despite those harsh realities?"

"Running a ranch can be tough," she admitted, "but I wouldn't have wanted to grow up anywhere else. How about you?"

"Delaware was fine, but actually I postponed a good part of my growing up until I joined the navy." His hard mouth lifted at the corners. "That's what guys off the Chesapeake do. Sign up when you're eighteen and see the world."

"Did you? See the world, I mean?"

"Not exactly. I was on submarine duty for two years, mostly up around the Arctic Circle."

She shivered reflexively. "Good Lord, that sounds dismal."

"It wasn't really. The situation was usually too tense to let the surroundings have much effect."

"What do you mean?" she asked.

"Even though people don't hear about it much, the Arctic Circle is where we tend to go head-to-head with the Soviets the most often. They're always testing us, we're always testing them. It's a constant game of chicken."

"Sounds wonderful," Jo said dourly. She was suddenly losing her appetite for what had been an excellent quenelle of salmon.

He shrugged. "That's the way the world works. Countries and people alike are out for whatever they can get."

"If I believed that," Jo said softly, "I wouldn't be able to get out of bed in the morning."

He had a sudden image of her doing exactly that and felt his body stir. Wryly he tried to push the thought aside, only to have it keep returning. That was awkward, to say the least. They were going to be working together, and he had a hard-and-fast rule never to get involved with anyone on a story.

Greeley was going to be a tough nut to crack, no doubt about that. But as he looked across the table at Jo, he had the definite impression that he was face-to-face with what would turn out to be both the most tantalizing and the most difficult part of his assignment.

He was silent for several moments as he gathered his thoughts. Quietly he said, "So you work for Greeley because you believe in him. Do you also believe he'll win?"

"He's the front-runner," Jo reminded him.

"Right now, and only for his party's nomination. Overall in the polls he's still losing. Besides, it's a long way to the convention, let alone the election itself. A lot can happen to change that or make it worse."

"That's true," she acknowledged. "But his positions are solid, he explains them well and people like him. He's touched a nerve with them."

"Has he? Or is it merely that he's gotten more coverage than most of the other candidates, so people simply tend to be more aware of him? You must know the theory that popularity polls are really based on no more than the recognition factor. If the public recognizes your name, they're more inclined to say they'd vote for you no matter what your policies may be."

"I hope you're wrong," Jo said quietly. "I know that a distressingly small percentage of qualified voters actually bother to vote, but I still think that they at least are conscientious about how they make their decisions. I don't believe they do it lightly."

"Maybe," David said, though it was clear that he remained doubtful. "At any rate, I think a good deal of the responsibility lies with the media. We often cover complex issues far too superficially." At her raised eyebrows, he laughed. "You're not used to hearing one of us admit it?"

"On the contrary," Jo said. "It seems to me that people in television are constantly beating their breasts, acknowledging their deficiencies and talking about how they have to do better. The problem is that they don't. You're right about the superficial coverage. That's what we were talking about earlier. Fifteen-second sound bites don't give much opportunity to get major ideas across. What I've never been able to understand is why it has to be that way?"

"It doesn't," David said quietly. "In case you haven't noticed, that isn't how I work."

Jo had noticed. She knew he was one of the very few people on network television who did thoughtful, in-depth reporting. When she knew he was going to be on, she actually made an effort to watch, which, under the circumstances, struck her as a bit humorous. Being part of David Wilson's audience was fine; being one of those he was scrutinizing was distinctly not.

She took a sip of her wine, glancing at him as she did so. The candle on the table cast his features into sharp relief. His broad, square-jawed face looked even more formidable than before. The flickering light gave him an almost primitive look that was accentuated by his thick hair, which was the color of beaten gold, and his uncompromisingly broad shoulders. He was a big man without a hint of softness, until she met his eyes and saw a glimmer there that she wasn't sure she wanted to recognize.

David Wilson was attracted to her. She acknowledged that simply, without vanity. She felt the same way about him. But under the circumstances it would be the height of foolhardiness to give in to that attraction.

Softly she said, "I meant what I said, you know."

"About our not being friends?" When she nodded, he smiled. She had the sense that he was far more amused by himself than by her. "In all the years I've been a reporter, I've never become personally involved with anyone I was covering."

"You say that rather regretfully."

"Not really. I never considered any alternative. I still don't want to." He lifted his glass to her. The wine sparkled in the candlelight, reflecting and magnifying the flame many times over. Quietly he said, "Whatever regret you hear is because I think I may have to now."

# Chapter 3

David insisted on seeing her home. Jo tried to convince him that it wasn't necessary, but he was having none of that.

"It's late," he pointed out as they left the restaurant where they had lingered for several hours. "Washington isn't the world's safest city. So let's not argue about it."

She gave in, admitting to herself that she wasn't in any hurry to part from him. Dinner had been surprisingly pleasant. She had managed, albeit with some difficulty, to push aside her worries over being attracted to him and where that might lead, and simply enjoy the moment.

He was a fascinating man, well-read, well traveled and with the intelligence to truly benefit from both. Moreover there was a genuineness about him that no doubt accounted at least in part for his success on television, that most intimate of media. For all his alleged cynicism, he truly cared about the quality of life for himself and for others.

If only they had met under different circumstances, she would have been looking forward to seeing him again. As it was, she would have to be on her toes to avoid forgetting exactly what it was that had brought them together.

"I don't believe this," Jo said as they got out of the taxi in front of her house. "It's raining again." Indeed, if the lowering sky was anything to go by, they were in for a long stretch of damp weather.

The glow of streetlights was reflected in dark pools of water along the brick sidewalk. Slender tree branches drooped limply. The wind whistling off the Potomac was fog laden and bone-deep chilling.

They ran the short distance to the door of Jo's building and huddled under the narrow lintel above the entrance as she searched for her key. She had just found it and was about to put it in the lock when a plaintive meowing reached them from somewhere nearby.

"What?" Jo murmured.

"Listen," David said, "there it is again."

"Poor thing, out on a night like this."

"It sounds like a kitten." He stepped away from the door and stood listening for a moment, then followed the weak, pitiful sound. Jo went after him, despite the rain that promptly began finding its way beneath the collar of her coat.

The building next to hers had a flight of stone steps leading up to its entrance. The sound was coming from beneath there.

"Wait here," David said as he bent slightly and stepped into the dark space. She heard him murmuring to something. A moment later, he emerged with a tiny, sodden kitten in his arms.

"He's soaked and madder than hell, not to mention terrified."

Jo had never been a cat person. There had always been plenty of kittens around the ranch, but she had a definite preference for dogs. Still, the abject creature tugged at her heart.

"You'd better bring him inside," she said as they returned to her building.

By the time they reached her apartment, the kitten was all but asleep in David's arms. Jo took off her raincoat and looked at the animal dubiously.

"We'll have to dry it off. I'll get a towel."

"Fine," David said. "Do you have any tuna fish, sardines, anything like that? Oh, and some old newspapers."

It took her several minutes to find everything he wanted. While she did, he dried the kitten gently and thoroughly. When Jo entered the kitchen with yesterday's newspaper and the bottom half of a cardboard carton, she was greeted by deep, throaty purrs.

Despite herself, she smiled. "All that noise from something so little?"

"He can't be more than a couple of months old," David said, stroking the kitten's back.

Jo bent over for a closer look. The kitten's fur was a mottled shade of orange, gray and brown. Still slightly damp, it appeared to stand on end. As she watched, the little cat opened its mouth and yawned hugely.

"It's falling asleep," she murmured.

"He should eat first. Here, hold him while I fix something."

Jo backed off slightly, but she wasn't fast enough. Before she could prevent it, the kitten was thrust into her hands. She held it awkwardly as David went over to the counter and opened the tin of tuna she'd left there. "Where are your plates?" he asked.

"In the cabinet above you. Do you think it'll be all right?"

"Should be if he has a place to stay."

"Well, since you found him . . ."

"Did I mention that I'm living in a hotel? I'm going to be based here permanently now that the nightly news is being anchored out of Washington, but I haven't found an apartment yet. Fact is, I haven't even had a chance to look."

Jo stifled a groan. "Let me guess, the hotel doesn't allow pets."

"A goldfish, maybe. Not a cat." He set the plate of tuna on the floor and went over to the refrigerator.

Jo couldn't help but notice that he seemed very comfortable in her home. "There's cream on the top shelf," she said a bit tartly.

"Perfect." He added some to a saucer and set that down beside the tuna. Meanwhile, the kitten had opened his eyes. At the smell of the food, he dug small sharp claws into Jo's arm.

"*Ouch*. He scratched me."

"Let me see," David said. He set the kitten down in front of the food and took her hand in his. "That's nothing much wrong, but you should wash it. He'll be better mannered when he isn't so hungry."

"You sound as though you think he's staying," she grumbled as he held her hand under the tap and ran warm water over it. As he did so, his fingers caressed hers gently. She thought of his hands touching the kitten with such care and a tremor raced through her. He would be a very tender lover.

At that thought, she flushed and tried to turn away. His fingers tightened around her. She felt the brush of his thigh against hers as he moved closer. "Jo... don't...."

She looked up, straight into the velvet darkness of his eyes. "We can't...."

"It's crazy...."

"Out of the ques—"

He hesitated a split second before lowering his mouth to hers. His lips were warm and gentle, the pressure they exerted exactly right, neither too little nor too much. He tasted of the fine French wine they had enjoyed at dinner. She breathed in the scent of him—crisp soap, sturdy wool and something else intrinsically his own. A soft, welcoming sigh escaped her as her lips parted.

His body, sensed through the civilizing layers of clothing, was pleasingly solid. She could feel the strength of his arms against her back as he drew her closer. His chest was broad and hard. She rested her hands against it as the kiss deepened.

Far in the back of her mind, Jo felt a spurt of surprise. The plain fact of the matter was that she had never really enjoyed kissing a man unless she knew him very well and felt a good deal of affection for him. Lacking that, the experience had always struck her as, at best meaningless, and at worst an unwelcome intrusion.

Though she lived in a very public world, she understood herself well enough to know that she was a very private person. It took a great deal to convince her to share any part of herself with a man. Which certainly did not explain why she was so delighted to be in David Wilson's arms, being thoroughly kissed.

He raised his head for a moment and looked down at her. Their eyes met, filled with the confusion and need they were both feeling. Jo's face was flushed, and her chestnut hair tumbled in disarray around her shoulders. Her lips were parted and moist. A low, purely male groan rumbled up out of David's chest as he gathered her to him again.

Jo hadn't reached the age of twenty-eight without being able to recognize when a situation was getting rapidly out of hand. Dazed as she was by David's kisses, she realized exactly where they were leading. Moreover she understood that if she was going to stop him, it had to be now.

Yet she hesitated. Never in her life had she been forced to wage so difficult a struggle between the rational and the passionate sides of her nature. She felt an almost physical wrenching when she finally mustered the strength of will to push him away.

"David, we have to stop." She had hoped to sound firm and resolute, but her voice was soft with a faint huskiness that was undeniably sensuous. For the briefest moment, she thought he was going to ignore her and persist. But in the next instant, he took a deep, shaky breath and let her go.

"You're right," he muttered, "I must be out of my mind to even think of making love with you."

For a man who made his living with words, Jo thought he could have put that better. Disappointment welled up in her, coming hard on regret. She had to fight against a sudden upsurge of tears that made her blink rapidly several times in succession.

"Nobody asked you to," she pointed out briskly. "This whole evening was supposed to be strictly business."

He ran a hand through his thick hair and smiled ruefully. "It hasn't quite worked out that way, has it?"

No man should be able to smile like that, she thought. It made him look utterly harmless, even endearing. It was absolutely ridiculous. She truly didn't believe she had ever met a more dangerous man.

"Let's forget this ever happened," Jo said. "We're both mature adults and professionals. There shouldn't be any reason why we can't work together perfectly well."

"Right. After all, it's only hormones. It would be a mistake to take it too seriously."

"I couldn't agree more," Jo said frostily. In another minute he was going to have her convinced that he passionately kissed every woman he met, and that none of them meant anything to him. Deep inside, she couldn't bear to believe he was that sort of man.

"I'll show you out," she said, not caring if that sounded rude. If he didn't leave soon, she was going to regret her resolution.

The kitten meowed again. David picked him up and petted him for a moment before handing him to Jo. "He still needs a place to stay."

She looked down into the small, delicately shaped face and sighed. "Oh, all right, I suppose I can keep him for a while. But it can't be permanent," she added hastily. "I'm not a cat person."

"You might be surprised," David said genially as he headed for the door. About to leave, he paused and glanced over his shoulder. "I'll see you at the office tomorrow."

Jo was startled to discover that she hadn't really given any thought as to how he intended to proceed with the story. She was taken aback as much by what she considered her own negligence as by the realization that she would be seeing him again so soon. The few hours between now and then didn't seem enough to gather together her composure and prepare to face him on a strictly impersonal level.

"So soon?" she murmured.

"Greeley's leaving on a campaign swing through the northeast in a few days, isn't he?" She nodded. "I presume you're going along?"

"For part of it. But I also have to mind the store here."

He hesitated, and she thought he was going to add something important, but after several moments he merely said, "Tomorrow, then."

After he had gone, Jo exhaled slowly. For a long time she stared at the door that had closed behind him, before finally remembering to lock it. Her mind seemed to have gone blank, overwhelmed by the problem of David Wilson.

That he was a problem she didn't doubt for a moment. The concerns she had felt when first learning that she was being assigned to work with him had doubled and tripled. He was far more of a threat than she could ever have imagined.

Around Congress, she had a well-earned reputation for always being cool under fire. The people who thought that of her would have laughed if they could have seen her just then. Cool was the last thing she felt after the onslaught of the fire David had lit within her.

She glanced at the clock on the kitchen wall and grimaced. "I've got nine hours to get myself into shape, cat. Think I can do it?"

Its only answer was a long feline yawn. With a laugh, she gently squeezed the kitten in her arms and took herself off to bed.

The rain continued into the predawn hours, turning the air damp and chilly. Sometime during the night, the kitten came up to the head of the bed and pawed at the covers. Jo roused herself drowsily, saw what it wanted and with a sigh let it under the blanket. It immediately curled against her tummy, where she felt the rumbling quiver of its purrs.

"Just don't get too comfortable, cat," she muttered. "This is strictly temporary."

Its only answer was the swipe of a raspy tongue against her fingers. With a smile, she drifted back into sleep.


Morning brought bright sunshine and a city washed clean. After making sure that the kitten had plenty to eat and a litter box filled with shredded newspaper, Jo left for work. She supposed she would have to pick up some basic supplies for the cat, but that could wait until she came home.

In the meantime, she had David to contend with. "He's starting this morning," she told Shelley in response to the inquiry she made the moment Jo walked into the office. "Apparently he wants to get a feel for how we operate, interview members of the staff, stuff like that."

"I think everyone is as well briefed as possible," Shelley said. "I got them together yesterday and explained that the great David Wilson was descending on us. I tried to stress the need to be cooperative but not gushy."

"I don't think we have to worry about our side. They all know the lay of the land."

"Then what are you worried about?" Shelley asked.

Jo grimaced slightly. "Is it that obvious?"

The older woman laughed. "You look fine, just a little tense. Not that I can blame you. Having to run interference between the senator and Wilson won't be any picnic."

"Maybe I won't really have to do that," Jo said.

Shelley raised her eyebrows. "You think Wilson's going to treat him with kid gloves?"

"No, of course not. But I'm hoping he'll at least be fair."

"I'm sure he will be, by his lights. But you have to realize that he doesn't get the ratings he does by telling America how great everything is. Face it, the public likes dirt. It's Wilson's job to dig it up."

"Then he's going to be disappointed," Jo said firmly. "The senator is clean, and so is this campaign."

"You and I know that," Shelley agreed. "The question is, will Wilson believe it?"

Jo frowned. "It's my job to convince him, isn't it?"

Shelley gave her a broad grin. "Better you than me, honey."

Jo hesitated a moment, then asked the question that had been on her mind ever since Greeley had assigned her to David. "Do you mind about this? I tried to convince the senator to give the job to you, but he was concerned about a conflict of interest between the office staff and the campaign. My salary's being paid by both, which I think is the only reason this has ended up in my lap."

Shelley shot her a quizzical look. "Is that really what you think?"

Jo nodded, puzzled by her colleague's surprise. After a moment, Shelley shrugged. "Look, let's be up-front about this. I do my job well and I'm proud of that, but I'm not the person to handle David Wilson. If it was some other TV hotshot, then sure, there wouldn't be any problem. That business with the salary is only a technicality anyway. I could switch payrolls easily enough."

"That's true," Jo said, realizing suddenly that Shelley was right.

Laughing, the older woman shook her head. "Don't get your hopes up. There's no way I'd suggest that to the senator, even if I thought he'd go for it, which he wouldn't. You've got what it takes to deal with Wilson. Nobody else here or on the campaign could do it as well."

"I don't understand why you say that," Jo said, genuinely baffled. "If anything, I'm going to have a harder time keeping my cool than a lot of other people would." That was so for more reasons than she cared to say, but among them was the fact that if David started sniping away at Greeley, she was going to be hard-pressed not to let him have it.

There was nothing wishy-washy about Jo's convictions. She believed intensely in the man she worked for, and she found it impossible to detach herself from attacks on him. If David made very many of the type of comments he had come out with in her office the previous day, holding on to her temper was going to be a problem.

Shelley looked at her directly and smiled. "You really don't get it, do you? Look, one of Greeley's great strengths is that he knows what makes people tick and how to get the best out of them, right?" When Jo nodded, she continued. "You and David Wilson happen to have a great deal in common, so it's natural for you to work together."

"In common?" Jo repeated. "He says rather proudly that he's a cynic while I own up, without embarrassment, to being something of an idealist. You call that having something in common?"

"Forget about the labels," Shelley advised. "Pay attention to what's under them instead. You both care, that's what it comes down to. David may tend to be more skeptical than you are, but that's his job. Have you ever heard anybody suggest that he isn't absolutely fair and honorable?"

"No," Jo admitted. With a grin, she added, "In fact, I've heard people complain about him for exactly those reasons."

"I've got news for you, honey. People say the same things about you." As Jo's eyes widened at the thought, Shelley said, "For heaven's sake, you are the most trusted aide of the man who may very well be the next president of the United States. Greeley relies on you like he does on nobody else in this staff or on the campaign. Sure, his family comes first with him, and he's also got some close friends he really trusts. But on a professional level, you're number one with him. Yet you have never once made use of that position for your own benefit. There aren't a lot of people around who could be in your shoes and make the same claim."

Jo thought about that for a while after Shelley went off to her own office. She had never considered herself in such terms. She simply had a job, and she did it to the best of her ability. But now that she reflected on it, she had to admit that there had been more times than she could count when somebody—a lobbyist, a constituent, another member of the Congressional staff—had attempted to ingratiate himself with her. That had become particularly the case as the senator rose in the polls and her own power, by association, increased.

There was never anything so overt as an actual bribe offered, but the intention was the same. If she had been willing to play along, she could have had her pick of speaking engagements with inflated fees in the thousands of dollars for a few hours' work, vacations at plush retreats presented in the guise of fact-finding expeditions, privileged insider information on stocks, and so on. It had never occurred to her to do so. She was aware of the practice and was thoroughly repelled by it.

David had a similar kind of strength, only in his case it came not from the ability to influence a single man, but to influence millions. Through television he reached directly into a very large percentage of the nation's homes. People listened to him and respected what he had to say. Had David wanted to, he could have availed himself of benefits even beyond what Jo was offered.

Shelley was right: they did have something in common. The problem was that, whether because of their similarities or through the simple vagaries of fate, they were very attracted to each other. That wouldn't do at all, Jo reminded herself, not at all.

With a conscious effort of will, she tried to put him out of her mind and attend to the numerous matters demanding her attention. While she managed to make headway with several of them, she didn't manage to banish him from her thoughts. He was still very much in them a half hour or so later when he strolled into her office.

He had dressed with the same casual elegance as he had the day before—dark slacks, a white turtleneck and a camel hair jacket. In the instant that she allowed herself to really look at him, Jo couldn't help but notice that he appeared tired and preoccupied. There was a slightly grim set to his mouth, and he had nicked himself while shaving. She caught herself wondering what was troubling him, told herself it was none of her business and murmured, "Good morning."

He gave her a cursory nod and got right to business. "What's on Greeley's agenda today?"

Jo was initially startled by his curtness, but quickly told herself that she ought to be relieved by it. If he had decided that any personal involvement between them was impossible, so much the better. It made everything much simpler. Simpler and safer. The kiss the night before had been a mistake; they both agreed on that. The sooner it was forgotten, the better.

Crisply she said, "He has a committee meeting this morning, then lunch with some constituents and a floor vote this afternoon. He's cleared time to talk with you after that, but he has to be out of here not later than six p.m. to get ready for a speaking engagement."

David stood with his hands in the pockets of his slacks. He looked faintly bored, but his thickly fringed brown eyes were very alert. She had the distinct impression that he was missing nothing. "Where's he speaking?"

Jo hesitated. She had debated whether or not to mention the engagement, but had finally decided that David would hear of it anyway. "It's a private meeting for key contributors."

"Does that mean it's closed to the press?" He no longer looked bored. Instead she could feel a definite surge of interest in him.

Carefully she said, "The people who will be attending would feel uncomfortable if a member of the media suddenly showed up."

He shrugged. "So it'll be off-the-record. Besides, I'm not dragging around cameras with me. That comes later."

"I'm still not sure...."

"Then ask. Tell Greeley I want to be there."

Despite all the promises Jo had made to herself not to let him get to her, she bridled. She had not come as far as she had by letting people run roughshod over her. It was time for David to understand that.

With deceptive softness she said, "You'll find that the peremptory approach doesn't work very well here. Not with members of this staff and certainly not with the senator himself. My instructions are to facilitate your access. That doesn't mean you get carte blanche."

David smiled faintly. "Are you saying I have to be a good little boy, or you'll send me home?"

Jo couldn't help but laugh. "Never in my wildest imagination would I dream of saying anything so foolish to you. If you're looking for an excuse to steamroller right over me, forget it. I'm not going to provide one. But you have to understand, and I'm sure you do, that we still have both a campaign and a senate office to run. The fact that you're on the scene doesn't change that."

"Why not?"

Jo looked at him blankly. "What do you mean?"

He took his hands out of his pockets, sat down in the chair opposite her desk he had occupied the day before and stretched out comfortably. It occurred to her suddenly that he took every possible moment to relax, which was wise in light of the hectic life he led.

"In my experience," he said, "public figures—especially those who happen to be running for president—will do anything for topflight media coverage. And I do mean *anything*. I did an in-depth report on one guy who skipped his grandmother's funeral rather than miss our deadline."

Genuinely shocked, Jo asked, "Couldn't you have extended it?"

"That's my point, I would have if he'd bothered to mention that she'd died, but all he could think about was the juicy coverage he was going to get on the eve of the election.''

"And did he?"

"Depends on what you mean by juicy. His was more a case of getting pulped."

Jo would have been less than human if she wasn't tempted to guess which politician he was talking about. She could think of one or two, maybe more, who fit the scenario.

"The senator's top priority is continuing to fulfill his responsibilities to his constituents," she said. "After that, admittedly a close second, comes the campaign."

"Uh-huh."

"It's true." Exasperated she said, "You're going to be disappointed when you realize what you're dealing with."

"You think so?"

"I know so. But you'll find out soon enough. In the meantime, I'd like to get a better idea of how you plan to proceed, who you want to talk with and so on."

"That's not really my style," he said blandly. "I just follow my nose."

"But arrangements have to be made...."

"Why?"

"So that people will know when they're supposed to speak with you and be available."

"I'm not wasting my time talking to people who are all primed and ready for me," he said. "I'd much rather catch them off guard."

"That's—"

"Tricky? Deceptive?" he suggested mockingly.

"No... actually, it's pretty smart. From your point of view, I mean. From mine, it's a pain in the..."

He grinned at her encouragingly. She shot him a chiding look in response and said primly, "In the neck. But I guess I'll just have to live with it."

"There are worse fates," he said agreeably.

"Offhand..."

"You can't think of one?"

"You'll save me a lot of time if you keep finishing my sentences like that."

"Sorry." He looked anything but contrite. In fact, he looked positively pleased with himself. She was still contemplating that when he asked, "How's the cat?"

The abrupt shift in gears took her a moment. "Uh... fine. He looked well fed and happy when I left."

"What did you name him?"

"I didn't. I told you, he's only temporary."

"Sure, sure, but he should have a name nonetheless."

Jo had a sudden inspiration born of some complex mixture of annoyance and fascination. "Let's see... he's already scratched me once, gotten fur all over my favorite sweater and hogged all the tuna. I think I'll name him Wilson."

She had the satisfaction of having surprised him, but then he bounced right back. "I'm honored." His voice dropped slightly as his eyes held hers. "Not to mention a little envious."

It was her turn to be surprised. "Why?"

He stood up to go, his hands back in his pockets and a teasing grin on his face. "Because, I'd be willing to bet where Wilson slept last night."

On that note, giving her no chance to reply, he departed.

# Chapter 4

Later in the afternoon Jo glanced up at the clock, saw what time it was and gave a little exclamation of surprise. As usual she had lost track of the hours. The day had proceeded at its customary breakneck speed. She had spent it on the phone, on the run and constantly on call.

As the senator's top aide, everyone knew to come to her with whatever business they felt needed immediate attention. She had lost count of the number of problems, situations and incipient crises she had juggled throughout the day, but she hadn't lost track of any of them. Each was stored away neatly in her copious memory, to be recalled whenever the need arose.

Only one thing was missing from her recollection of the hectic day, and that was David Wilson. He had been conspicuous only by virtue of the low profile he had maintained. Their paths had crossed from time to time, and she had been dimly aware of him speaking with various people. But he made no attempt to talk with her again, nor did he make any demands on her time or attention.

That annoyed her vaguely, though she told herself to be grateful for small favors. If the rest of his coverage went even half as smoothly, they would be home free.

Before leaving the office shortly after five p.m., she spoke with several staff members who had been interviewed by David. They both expressed relief that he hadn't been anywhere near as tough or probing as they had expected.

"He really couldn't have been nicer," a young secretary named Cindy said brightly. "After a few minutes, I felt so relaxed talking to him. He seems so tough on television, but in person he's nothing at all like that."

Jo managed a faint smile. She supposed that Cindy would be saying those same words to anyone she could find to listen. Being interviewed by David Wilson was impressive enough, but being able to tell her friends that she knew what he was really like added considerably to the experience.

It was on the tip of her tongue to ask the young girl what she had told him, but Jo stopped herself. She did not want anyone on the staff to feel unable to speak openly with David. Simple decency dictated that, but in addition, if he suspected they were in any way being censored, she had no doubt how he would react.

She was still thinking about David and his interviewing techniques as she left the Senate office building and strolled to the bus stop. A steady stream of

traffic passed her, limousines mixed with private cars
belonging to those who took advantage of the parking spaces that were a perquisite of their jobs.

Jo could have done the same, but her idea of driving was to get out on an empty highway, find a really
good country music station on the radio, roll the windows all the way down and sing along. It was most
decidedly not going bumper-to-bumper with half of
Washington.

As she left the bus at the other end and walked the
few blocks to her apartment, she almost regretted
having to go out again that evening. Much as she hated
to admit it, Jason wasn't the only one feeling worn
down by the campaign. She had begun to have fanta-
sies about stretching out on a white-sand beach with
nothing to do except turn over occasionally.

Given her busy schedule, such relaxation would be
a long while coming. But she still wished there was
some way to snatch even a little time from her job.
Being out with David the night before had reminded
her of what little private life she had. Everything she
did, everyone she saw seemed to be tied in one way or
another to her job.

That evening was no exception. A glance at her
watch—right side up this time—told her that she had
less than an hour to get ready for the contributors'
dinner. She was hurrying as she pulled her mail out of
the box and unlocked the front door.

"Always rushing," a gentle voice said as she eased
herself inside, trying to balance her briefcase, pocketbook and the pile of mostly junk mail. "Here, let me
give you a hand."

"Thanks," she said with a smile. The elderly man who had just stepped out of his own ground-floor apartment smiled in return. Francis MacInnes would not see seventy again, but his bearing and manner were more youthful than that of many men half his age. He stood a shade under six feet tall, had thinning silver hair and the long, slightly horsey features of an aristocrat.

It was a source of pride to him that he still weighed exactly what he had a quarter of a century before when he had been United States ambassador to Luxembourg. That posting had been only one in a long and distinguished career of service to his country.

The heir to a considerable New England shipping fortune, he had bought the Georgetown town house fifty years before. Despite the death of his wife and the inevitable departure of their four children who went off to make their own lives, he had never seen any reason to move.

Five years earlier he had surprised his friends by converting the upper floor of his residence into a separate apartment and declaring his intention to rent it out. There had been a brief flurry of concern that perhaps Francis's financial situation wasn't as ample as everyone had presumed. But in fact he had been motivated solely by a desire for company. He had gotten what he wanted in the form of Jo Blakely who became tenant, friend and to a very large extent, adopted daughter.

"Busy day?" Francis asked as he helped relieve her of her burdens. He continued to practice an old world courtesy that dictated the holding of doors, carrying of parcels and other sadly outdated kindnesses.

"About as usual," Jo said. "It certainly isn't going to get any easier before this is over."

"Jason holding up all right?"

Jo nodded. They climbed the stairs to her apartment without Francis becoming in the least winded. Granted, he took the steps slowly, but he showed no aftereffects of the pneumonia that had laid him low during the winter and worried her terribly.

She was extremely fond of Francis. Both of her own grandfathers had died while she was a small child, and she could barely remember them. Francis filled a gap in her experience of people.

In less hectic times she had spent delightful evenings with him, listening to his reminiscences about times and places that would otherwise have been the dry stuff of history books to her. She knew that he appreciated her company, and that feeling was fully reciprocated. One of her very few regrets about the campaign was that it was now impossible for her to see him as often as she would have liked.

"The senator is doing very well under the circumstances," she said as she opened her apartment door. "He's looking forward to meeting with you next weekend."

Francis had become an important adviser to the Greeley campaign, particularly on foreign affairs for which he continued to have a definite flair. "I've gone over the draft of the position paper he intends to release. There are several issues which I believe need to be redefined."

Jo nodded. She, too, had seen the draft and had not been satisfied with it. She was about to say so when a small, furry projectile launched itself directly at her, coming to rest in the middle of her chest to which it clung with fiercely sharp little claws.

"What on earth—" Francis began.

"Wilson," Jo moaned. She had dropped her handbag at the shock of so exuberant a greeting and now bent to retrieve it, meanwhile trying to disengage the kitten from her jacket and blouse. Her efforts were greeted by frantic purrs and several loving swipes with a rough tongue.

"I had no idea you were fond of cats," Francis said, his eyes twinkling as he observed her attempts to cope with so much feline affection.

"Neither did I," Jo muttered. "But don't worry, this one's only temporary."

The former ambassador's abundant eyebrows rose. "Really? He seems to think otherwise."

Persuaded at last to release her, Wilson sat down on the carpet at Jo's feet and busily began to wash himself. He looked up at Francis as he spoke, blinked once and returned to the job at hand.

"I've always been rather partial to cats myself," Francis said as he smiled at the kitten fondly.

"Then perhaps you'd like this one," Jo suggested hastily.

"Oh, I think he'll do nicely here. However I will look after him for you when you're away."

"Thanks," Jo said resignedly. She hated to admit it, but she had been worried about what would happen to Wilson when she had to be on the road with the campaign. The sensible thing would have been to find him another home, but despite her suggestion to Francis, she was less eager to part with the kitten than she tried to pretend. Not, of course, that her reluc-

tance had anything to do with who had found him or
who he happened to be named for.

"Have a good time this evening," Francis said as he
turned to leave. He was aware of the contributors'
dinner, and had in fact introduced the senator to several of those who would be attending. He had been
invited but had demurred, saying that at his age a
brandy and a good book were preferable to all the
trappings of official Washington.

Jo had to agree with him as she fed Wilson, then
quickly darted into the shower. Half an hour later she
was zipping up the back of her evening dress and slipping her feet into high-heeled slippers. One of the ad-
vantages to be had from short, curly hair was that it
didn't lend itself to anything fancy. A few swipes with
the brush were enough to whip it into shape for the
evening.

Some time ago Jo had decided that since she seemed
destined for a very busy life, lived to a large degree in
the public spotlight, she would be wise to learn how to
look her best with a minimum of time and effort. The
makeup consultant she had gone to see had designed
two basic routines for her, one for daytime and another, slightly more elaborate one for evening.

The evening style emphasized her large, expressive
gray eyes, her high cheekbones and the soft fullness of
her mouth. Small diamond earrings that were a gift
from her family added the proper note of elegance
without being ostentatious. A spray of her favorite
freesia-based scent, a strand of pearls put around her
throat, and she was ready to go.

Before leaving she paused to check Wilson's milk
and food dishes. He seemed to expect more, so she

gave him a little scratch behind the ears. That set off rapturous purring, which made her feel obligated to keep on petting him for at least another few minutes. Only when she realized that she was smiling broadly at the little kitten's antics, and that he seemed ready to go on like that all night, did she reluctantly break it off.

"I have to go out, Wilson," she said, feeling not quite right about walking away without a word. "Uh...don't break anything, okay? And take care of yourself."

He blinked solemnly, curled up on top of the dishwasher and began to give himself a thorough wash. Satisfied that he would be fine on his own, Jo left, but not without a backward glance that made her shake her head.

Who said people were smarter than cats? There she was, going out to what she fully expected would be, at best, a tedious evening when what she really would have liked to do was to get through some of her excess paperwork and go to bed.

So much for expectations. Barely had Jo arrived at the private club discreetly situated on a quiet back street when she began to suspect that something was not quite right. Glancing around the Georgian-style entry hall, she saw nothing that might have set off her trouble detector, yet it was ringing loud and clear. Puzzled, she took another, more careful look as she smiled and nodded to the arriving guests.

Introductions were hardly necessary since everyone knew everyone else. That was quite customary at the level of wealth and power from which the guest list had been assembled. Conversations took up more or less where they had left off the day before or several months ago. Most of those present were men, dressed as expected in formal evening wear.

There was a scattering of women, generally middle-aged and older but so beautifully gowned and well cared for that age was hardly an issue with them. Some were wives of the men attending; others were widows who controlled substantial wealth.

One or two stood out from the crowd, at least in Jo's mind, because they were women who had made their own fortunes. She nodded to the founder of an enormously successful cosmetics line and exchanged a few words with the president of the only woman-run investment firm on Wall Street.

All the while she felt the wash of nervous energy that invariably warned her something was about to happen. Yet everything seemed perfectly in order.

The senator arrived, accompanied by his wife. Marianne Greeley looked lovely, as always, her petite, blond beauty perfectly set off by a gown of mauve silk. Jo was certain that almost no one would notice the faint shadows beneath the older woman's hazel eyes.

When she had a moment, Jo worked her way over to where Marianne was standing and murmured, "I'm glad you could make it this evening. How is Hilary feeling?"

The senator's wife gave her a wan smile. "Better, I think. She was sleeping soundly when I left, thank heavens."

Jo didn't have to be told that, had there been any doubt about how the little girl was doing, her mother would not have left her, nor would the senator have tried to get her to do so. There were those who criticized Marianne Greeley, out of her husband's hearing, for not putting his presidential campaign above all else. Jo thought, and didn't mind saying, that the other woman's priorities were perfectly correct.

"I'm glad," she said as she accepted a glass of white wine from a passing waiter. As usual at such functions, there would be an hour or so of cocktail chitchat before the guests went in to dinner. Following that, the senator would give a talk about his policies and then open the floor to questions.

No one would be so tactless as to mention money, but it was understood that the purpose of the evening was to encourage financial support. Keeping the Greeley campaign afloat financially was more difficult than it might have been because the senator refused to accept donations from what he regarded as pressure groups set up specifically to buy friends in high places. As a result he was perpetually trying to catch up with his campaign debt, despite his popularity in the polls.

Marianne Greeley must have been thinking about that when she laughed under her breath and murmured, "Looks like a good group. I can practically hear the checkbooks rustling."

"They smell a winner," Jo said. She didn't delude herself that everyone invited to the gathering was a fervent Greeley supporter. Many of them didn't so much agree with his policies as simply didn't care.

If he wanted to get excited about the need to improve public education and to rebuild the economy, fine. What counted with them was that once he was elected, he would remember who had helped pay the bills.

Most of them would never actually ask for anything from him except the right to drop his name familiarly, hang an inscribed photo on the wall and occasionally put through a call that would be taken by a respectful White House assistant who would promise to relay their messages to the president. Only a very few of them would appear on the list of those Greeley himself would be willing to talk to.

Jo took another sip of her wine and glanced toward the door, in time to see one of those few arrive. Elizabeth Stewart had been a fixture on the Washington political scene for some forty years, ever since she had come to the capital as a young bride of twenty-five. Time had turned her sleekly coiffed hair white and slightly thickened her slender body, but it had done nothing to lessen the bright gleam of intelligence and interest that lit her brown eyes, nor to diminish the smile of anticipation that raised the corners of her mouth as she surveyed her fellow guests.

Jo was just about to move forward when her gaze suddenly fell on the man standing next to Elizabeth, and she gasped softly. David Wilson, had, for once, forsworn his customarily casual dress, with devastating results. Jo found him disturbing enough in regular clothes; in formal evening wear he was ruthlessly attractive. His appearance did not, however, change the fact that he had absolutely no business being where he was.

Her mouth set in a dangerously firm line, Jo crossed the distance between them and confronted him directly. "What a surprise to see you here, David. I thought it was understood that you wouldn't be attending?''

Instead of responding he merely smiled and inclined his head. "Good evening, Jo, nice to see you, too." He turned to Elizabeth, who was observing them both keenly. "I believe you two know each other?"

Jo managed a stiff nod. "Good evening, Mrs. Stewart. It's nice to see you again."

"And you, my dear. Don't let my nephew's being here disturb you. He's absolutely promised to forget he's a reporter for the duration of the evening."

Jo couldn't help herself. She cast him a blatantly skeptical look, even as she grappled with the fact that he was Elizabeth Stewart's nephew. How that particular piece of information had managed to escape her, she didn't know.

Not that it made any real difference. He was there, and there was nothing she could do about it, short of making a scene and undoubtedly angering one of the senator's most important supporters.

"If you say so, Mrs. Stewart," she said as confidently as she could manage.

The cocktail hour was winding down, and the guests were beginning to drift into the dining room. She shot David a warning glance that she hoped told him she expected his aunt's assurances to be upheld. His only response was an ingenuous smile that did nothing at all to reassure her.

"We'd be delighted if you would sit with us, my dear," Elizabeth Stewart said. Jo could hardly refuse her. She nodded a shade glumly, which brought a twinkle of amusement to the older woman's eyes.

Gallantly David offered each an arm. The three made their way into the dining room, which was rapidly filling up with guests.

One of the reasons the private club had been chosen as the site for the dinner was that it offered better food than was customary at such events. Jo personally had nothing against chicken, mashed potatoes and peas. She had grown up on such food. But that didn't mean she cared to have it every night. On the political circuit it was not only possible to do so, it was almost unavoidable.

Jo had lost count of the time she had spent cooling her heels in hotel lobbies simply because she couldn't stand to face the food at dinner. She hadn't been alone on such occasions, either. As she had pointed out to the senator, a good case could be made that more went on behind the scenes than at the event itself. One of her fondest memories was of sharing a fast-food hamburger and fries with an elderly gentleman who also had an aversion to what he aptly called library paste cuisine.

They had chatted about everything from whether or not the New York Mets would ever pull out of their slump to Greeley and his policies. Two days later the campaign had received a check from the gentleman and a pledge of further support.

Only then had Jo discovered that he was one of the most influential men in the country. She had felt embarrassed by her own lack of awareness until Jason explained that there was a number of people like him who studiously preserved their anonymity and resisted any attempts to gain their support through the usual channels. They preferred to make up their own minds without what they considered to be undue interference. Jo couldn't help but admire them.

But she was glad that none of those attending the present affair had the same attitude. They were either already Greeley supporters or very inclined to become so. Nonetheless they expected a good show for their efforts and they weren't disappointed.

The chef who had prepared that night's dinner didn't hold with anything so trendy as nouvelle cuisine. He was a proponent of classical French cooking, and Jo had to admit he made it very difficult not to think that everything invented since was an aberration.

Over a meal of lobster bisque, scallops of veal with foie gras and truffles, and a walnut cake with apricot filling, Jo decided that losing ten pounds really wasn't all that important after all. As she savored a particularly tasty bite of the cake, so delectable that she closed her eyes in delight, she reflected that she liked herself the way she was, and that there was really no reason to change.

In the back of her mind, refusing to be silent, a little voice pointed out that David seemed to like her just fine, too. She sternly told herself that didn't matter, and tried to believe it.

## Chapter 5

Elizabeth's an interesting woman," David said as he swirled the brandy in his crystal snifter and watched the firelight reflected in the amber liquid. "She never does anything without a reason."

Curled up in a chair across from him, Wilson in her lap, Jo nodded slowly. "It must run in the family."

David's eyebrows rose fractionally. "Why do you say that?"

"Because I'm still not sure what you're doing here. I had every intention of coming home alone."

"I should hope so. Most of the men at this evening's little get-together were old enough to be your father."

"You know perfectly well what I mean. I had no intention of seeing you again outside of the line of duty. But when you sidled up as I was leaving and—"

"I did not sidle," David said self-righteously. "I never sidle."

Jo ignored him. "And put on your best Boy Scout look."

His mouth twisted with amusement. "My what?"

"That innocent look you have, the one you use when you want everyone to believe that you have absolutely nothing in mind except doing a good deed or maybe winning another merit badge."

"Oh, *that* look. Go on."

"Right in front of the senator and your aunt, both of whom jumped on your suggestion that I shouldn't be out after dark by myself. That's the second time you've used that, you know. I hope you aren't going to try to make a habit of it. It makes me sound as though I'm eight years old."

David laughed softly. He took a sip of his brandy and relaxed against the couch. He was enjoying watching her. She looked very lovely, curled up in the oversize chair with her shoes kicked off, and her feet tucked under her.

He supposed she had no idea that her sedate little black dress was twisted around her just enough to reveal the high, full curve of her breasts and the slenderness of her waist. With many other women of his acquaintance, he would have suspected a certain degree of contrivance. But Jo was different: she didn't have the time or the interest to play such games. In a city where subterfuge was as commonplace as Potomac River fog, she was refreshingly straightforward.

She was also very tired. Her shoulders drooped slightly and her eyes had a heavy-lidded look he found

disturbingly arousing. "I should go," he murmured
without making any attempt to stand up.

Jo nodded. "That's right, you should. Would you
care for more brandy?"

His smile deepened. "That's a contradiction."

"So are you." She shook her head. "I don't know
what I'm saying. I shouldn't be talking to you at all."

He put his brandy snifter down on the table beside
the couch. "You really are tired."

Jo sighed and closed her eyes for a moment. "Is
that ever the truth. I've decided that politics is very
Darwinesque. Only the fittest survive. Oh..." Her eyes
opened, and she attempted to twist around, only to be
stopped by firm hands on her shoulders. "What are
you doing?"

"Rubbing the back of your neck." David had risen
and was standing behind her chair. His long fingers
touched her with exquisite firmness. He seemed to
know exactly where her muscles were knotted and how
to loosen them.

Before she could stop herself, a sound not unlike
one of Wilson's best purrs broke from her. "Oh, that
feels good."

"Hmm. Lean forward a little."

She did as he said and was rewarded by the delectable sensation of his thumbs pressing lightly along the
ridge of her spine. "I think I could die from this," she
murmured.

He laughed softly. "Don't worry. I'll stop before
then."

She wasn't sure she wanted him to. Wilson, feeling
himself cramped, jumped off her lap and stalked

away. Jo barely noticed. Her awareness was narrowing down to David, his nearness and his touch.

"Shiatsu," she said.

"Bless you."

"I meant the massage. It reminds me of Japanese shiatsu. Have you ever had that?"

"No."

"I have, twice. It's wonderful. You just sort of dissolve...like now...."

"Jo, be quiet."

"Wha—?"

"You don't have to talk. You don't have to be nervous. Everything is all right."

"Easy for you to say," she grumbled.

"Wanna bet?"

"I hate it when you mumble."

"I said," he spoke very clearly, "that if you think this is easy for me, you're crazy. I am trying very hard to be nice, helpful, a gentleman, all that sort of thing. But inside..."

"Don't stop now. You're just getting to the interesting part."

She felt the low tremor of his amusement as he bent closer to her, the warmth of his large body touching her almost as his hands did. "You get very reckless when you're tired. Did you know that?"

"I'm never reckless," she informed him firmly. "Ask anyone. Good old methodical Jo."

"If you say so. Inside," he went on, dropping his voice a notch, "a ravening beast demanding to be let out."

Despite herself Jo giggled. "What's funny?" David demanded.

"You sound like I imagine Wilson will when he learns how to growl."

He was silent a moment before he came around to the front of the chair and knelt before her. An instant later she felt the brush of his lips against her throat. "Sweetheart," he murmured, "one thing I'm not is a pussycat."

His mouth searched for hers slowly, enticingly, touching off fire storms of pleasure everywhere it lingered. Jo tangled her fingers in his thick, crisp hair and held on for dear life.

Everything about the man was new and fascinating, especially what he made her feel. Oh, what he made her feel. Reborn, new, utterly unafraid. Crazy.

"Crazy," she whispered, drinking in the scent of him, engulfed by sensation, dizzied by need.

"Insane," he agreed as his heart hammered against his ribs. He was a man who prided himself on his self-control in even the most difficult situations. The whole world might be going mad, but David Wilson kept his cool. Except that the soft, slender woman in his arms had thrown him into overdrive, and he was suddenly in very real danger of overheating.

He was on the verge of deciding that there were worse fates when he suddenly focused on her face, lying white and strained against his broad shoulder. Her eyes were luminous, her lips moist and parted.

She was as caught up in what was happening between them as he was. Of that he was certain. But she was also very vulnerable. He could feel the weariness in her warring with the arousal he had provoked. Her body lay in his arms as trustingly as a child might.

"Damn it," he muttered.

Jo's eyes flew open. "What?"

"It's going on two a.m. We both have to be at work in the morning. You're worn out, and I'm not far from it. That isn't how it should be between us, if it should be at all."

His frankness recalled Jo to herself with brutal effectiveness. She felt as though she had been tossed from a cozy warm nest into an ice-cold bath. Her whole body stiffened as she pushed away from him and sat up. "No, it isn't. I don't know what's wrong with me. The mere idea that you and I would..." She broke off, unable to go any further.

David had no such scruples. His face hardened as he rose and looked down at her. "Would make love? We already were and in another moment or two we would have been going a lot further."

"But we've stopped, and we aren't going to start again, so that's that." Holding on to the side of the chair, hoping that he wouldn't notice how shaky she was, she stood up. It was going to take all her strength to see him to the door, but she was going to do it. And fast. Because if she hesitated even briefly, she would forget all her resolve.

"So tidy," he said, "so controlled. Do you really think you can keep that up?"

"Yes," she said firmly. "Because I have to. The only alternative is completely unacceptable. Can you honestly tell me that we can become lovers and still do our jobs effectively?"

David hesitated a long moment. Almost everything in him wanted to assure her of exactly that. Only one thing stopped him—the innate honesty that refused to let him lie to either himself or her.

"No," he said finally, "I can't tell you that. We'd be in a hell of a mess. I have to retain my objectivity in order to do the story properly. And you..."

"I have to remember that your priorities are not the same as my own," she finished for him. "If we aren't adversaries, we're the next thing to it."

He looked at her intently as though seeking to memorize exactly how she looked at that moment. Slowly the harsh tautness of his features eased. "This campaign won't last forever."

"That's true," she said, secretly pleased that he would be willing to wait until it was over to pursue her. But the pleasure was dimmed by a commonsense understanding of reality. "Emotions can't really be put on hold, can they? They either have to be allowed to run free and grow, or they wither away."

He shook his head wryly. "You would have made it a lot easier for me to leave if you'd agreed with me."

Jo blinked several times against the sudden burning in her eyes. "I'm sorry. Oh, I really am. But if we can't be anything else, I think we should at least be honest with each other."

He could hardly argue with that, particularly since he admired the courage that made her face up to so unpleasant a truth. He was having trouble doing that himself.

Even though he knew she was right about the impossibility of putting emotions on hold, he wanted to believe that there was still a chance for them. Wanted it so much that it scared him.

Long after he got back to his hotel room, he lay awake thinking about her and the effect she had on him. The bottom line was that he simply couldn't afford an involvement. His job came first, not simply for his sake but for what it represented.

As unfashionable as it might sound, he took his responsibilities very seriously. He had a duty to search for and reveal the truth. Moreover he was good at it. Damn good. Certainly better than many of his colleagues who were all too often either content with media handouts or simply misled by highly skilled front men. Front persons. Whatever. People like Jo, charged with protecting those in power and promoting the most desirable image of them to the public.

There was no vanity in his recognition that he did his job well; he evaluated his own performance as relentlessly as he did anyone else's. Both by intellect and by inclination, he had the ability to dig beneath the surface and get to the essence of who a particular person really was. He considered the privacy of ordinary people to be absolutely sacrosanct, but believed exactly the opposite for those who aspired to power.

Jason Greeley wanted to be president of the United States. Jo Blakely wanted to help put him there. David Wilson wanted people to know who they might be voting for before they did so. Really know.

Occasionally in the past, unqualified men had achieved the highest office by dint of politicking, fate or just plain dumb luck—theirs, not the country's. America had always managed to muddle through. But in the nuclear age, on the eve of the third millennium, the stakes were simply too high.

David turned over in bed, feeling the sheets pull at his long, bare legs. He slept naked winter and summer, disliking the confinement of pajamas. With an exclamation of irritation, he kicked the covers off.

The only warmth he wanted to feel was of Jo's body against his own. Lacking that, and facing the prospect of that lack extending forever, he couldn't help but give into the selfish wish that she was as uncomfortable as he himself.

She could have told him, had she known, that his wish was granted. Jo slept poorly, tossing and turning through the few hours until her alarm clock went off. She wanted nothing so much as to hide her head under the pillow, but instead she crawled out of bed and did her best to whip herself into shape and face the new day.

At least the sun was shining. Telling herself to be grateful for small favors, she arrived at the office early, for once getting in ahead of the senator. He was departing on a campaign swing through the northeast that morning and would be dropping by the office for only a few minutes before leaving.

Jo spent a long phone call explaining that fact to the officious assistant of one of Greeley's senatorial colleagues. The aide kept insisting that he absolutely had to see Greeley that day.

"I'm sorry," she said patiently, "but the senator won't be available. However if you'd like to tell me what the problem is, I'll do my best to take care of it."

"That's unacceptable," the young man snarled over the phone line. His office was only at the other end of the hall from Jo's, but it would not have occurred to him to drop by to see her rather than to call. Matters of territory and the vital question of who came to whom were always uppermost in the minds of such people.

"We have to speak with the senator himself. He'll simply have to find the time. If you don't make that clear to him, there'll be hell to pay."

High on Jo's list of things she didn't like were people who referred to themselves as *we.* Also right up there were arrogant, pushy browbeaters who counted on intimidation to get them what they wanted. In the case of the young man, she suspected that he merely wanted to test out his clout—and his boss's—on the leading presidential candidate. It wasn't going to work.

Gently but firmly, Jo said, "I'd like to help, but what you're asking is impossible. Unless you can tell me that there is a genuine emergency that absolutely requires the senator's attention, his schedule stands as is."

"Now look—" the young man began.

"No," Jo broke in, "you look. We both know that if something serious was cooking, I'd have heard about it, so let's stop playing games. If your man wants to see Greeley, fine. I'll clear some time later in the week. But you can't get him in here today, and that's final."

The young man was still blustering a few minutes later when Jo disengaged herself and hung up. It never failed to amaze her how men who should know better simply could not understand when a woman refused to knuckle under and do what they wanted. Men such as the one she had just tussled with expected women to do things they would never even think of asking another man to do. Jo had no compunction whatsoever about showing them that they were wrong.

She was still shaking her head over the encounter when a secretary stuck her head in the door and whispered, "Mrs. Stewart is here. What should I do?"

Jo's reactions were normally faster than those of most people, but for an instant she was stymied. Wealthy supporters did occasionally show up at the senator's office unannounced, but she couldn't remember Elizabeth Stewart ever having done so.

That was enough to make her think twice about what she should do, but added to it was the instant flow of thought that the woman's arrival set off. Jo had managed to get through most of the morning without thinking about David, but that ended abruptly the moment she realized that his aunt was waiting in the anteroom.

"I'll see her," she said, rising quickly. Elizabeth Stewart had declined the chair the secretary had offered her. She was standing with her back to Jo, examining one of the watercolors hanging on the walls. As she turned, she said, "Marianne is a gifted artist. I hope she'll be able to continue painting once she becomes First Lady."

"I'm sure she plans to," Jo said. Her unexpected visitor was elegantly garbed in a beige wool suit Jo recognized as being by Chanel. Elizabeth's silver hair was drawn up in a chignon set off by a small hat. Pearls large enough to be fake, but which happened to be real, graced her ears. She was the epitome of the wealthy, fashionable woman, except that her brown eyes danced with a liveliness many such women lacked.

"Do forgive me for dropping in like this," she said with a gentle smile. "I hope it isn't a great inconvenience?"

"Not at all," Jo assured her, "but I'm afraid you've missed the senator. He took off this morning for a campaign swing."

"Yes, I know. David went with him. Actually it's you I wanted to see."

Jo couldn't imagine why, but she could hardly say that. Instead she murmured, "Of course, if there's anything I can do for you...."

"You can indulge an old lady and keep her company at lunch. That is, if you have no other plans?"

"Why no, I'd be delighted." Not for a moment did Jo believe that Elizabeth merely wanted someone to have lunch with. Had that been the case, she could have chosen from among literally hundreds of friends and acquaintances in the capital, all of whom would have been more than happy to oblige her.

Into her mind popped what David had said the night before about his aunt never doing anything without a reason. Jo had the feeling that she would shortly find out what that might be.

"I didn't know David had gone with the senator," she said as she slipped into the turquoise suede jacket that matched the skirt she had put on that morning. With it she wore a jade silk shirt and a silver-and-turquoise belt. The outfit was hardly regulation dress-for-success attire, but Jo absolutely refused to adopt the mannish clothing some ambitious women felt compelled to wear. She was glad to be a woman and didn't mind who knew it.

They left the building and stepped out into the bright sunshine of what promised to be an unusually pleasant day. A vintage Rolls-Royce was parked at the curb with a uniformed driver who promptly jumped out to open the door for them.

"Thank you, Ferguson," Elizabeth said as she stepped into the luxuriously appointed back seat. "We'll be lunching at Papillon's."

As the car pulled away from the curb, Jo settled into the plush leather upholstery and gave herself up to the sensation of total ease. After a moment she murmured, "It's true what they say."

"What's that?" Elizabeth asked.

"That the loudest sound in a Rolls-Royce is the ticking of the clock. If I didn't know better, I'd swear this thing had wings instead of an engine."

The older woman chuckled. "You know, my dear, there are a great many people who wouldn't dream of revealing that they hadn't ridden in a Rolls before. You're rather refreshingly frank."

"It takes too much energy to be anything else," Jo said dryly. She was beginning to relax and feel more at ease with the formidable lady at her side. Elizabeth reminded her in many ways of David. Both had a keenly intelligent, perceptive approach to the world that she couldn't help but admire.

"I had no idea that you and David were related," she said. "It really threw me when he turned up at the dinner last night."

"So I gathered," Elizabeth said with a smile. "It threw him when I asked him to go along."

"You asked . . . ?"

"You presumed he had wangled his way in?"

"Well . . . yes, I admit I did."

"Oh, I'm sure the idea occurred to him, but as good a reporter as he is, David has always known where to draw the line at antagonizing people. He understood when you said the guests would probably be made uncomfortable by his presence."

"He told you that?"

Elizabeth nodded. "When he asked me if I'd ever met you. He knows, you see, that I'm a Greeley supporter so he thought we might have encountered each other."

"I can't imagine why he cared whether or not you had met me."

The older woman smiled. "I would imagine he wanted to ask me about you, which was what led me to decide it was time the two of us got better acquainted. You know, David is very dear to me. I have no children of my own, and I've always considered him as a son, even when he was getting in all those scrapes."

Jo was beginning to realize Elizabeth had a habit of dropping not one but several fascinating little tidbits all at once so that her listeners hardly knew which to pick up first. Start at the beginning, Jo decided, and she proceeded to do exactly that as the elegant car whisked them across the Potomac and into Virginia.

## Chapter 6

Such a pleasant place," Elizabeth said as the two women strolled together along the gravel path that led past formal gardens to a stately antebellum mansion. Robins twittered in the flowering magnolia trees, and a blue jay squawked at them as they passed. The scent of daffodils, flowering lavender and irises followed in their wake.

"It's difficult to believe we're so close to the city," Jo said. "This could be another planet."

"It might as well be," Elizabeth agreed. "Did you know it was almost torn down a few years ago? We're so wasteful of our heritage, as though we had a great deal of it, when in fact we have anything but."

"At least it's safe now. From what I hear, Papillon's is very much a going concern." Glancing around, Jo was more convinced of that than ever. Unlike the private club where she had been the night before,

Papillon's had nothing of the masculine imprint that so characterized the nation's capital. It was unabashedly feminine, from the entry hall's beautiful curved mahogany staircase to the twin terraces on either side of the main building that were half enclosed by trellises of honeysuckle and rose.

Men were not precisely barred from Papillon's— that would have been illegal—but they were hardly encouraged, either. In addition to the restaurant there was a luxurious spa and beauty salon, which ensured that any man who did happen to wander in, quickly felt out of place.

"I'll be interested to know what you think of it," Elizabeth said as they took their places on the terrace. They were seated at a simple pine table covered with fluttering lace and set with blue-and-white faience plates. Blue-stemmed glassware and silver continued the country French motif that characterized all of Papillon's.

"It's so cool," Jo said, "and refreshing. This place must be particularly wonderful in the summer."

"When Washington is so particularly dreadful. But then if the weather was more pleasant, Congress might be tempted to stay in session, and that certainly wouldn't do the country any good."

Jo laughed. "That's what the senator says, too. I worry sometimes that he's going to trip over his own irreverence before this campaign is over."

"I wouldn't be too concerned if I were you, dear. Jason is a very clever man. He understands that one of the things the voters like most about him is that he doesn't seem to take himself too seriously."

"I hope David will pick up on that and understand it. He worries me with his cynicism."

"Perhaps you wouldn't be so concerned if you knew where it comes from." Elizabeth took a sip of the Campari that had been placed before her by a discreet waiter. Jo was making do with club soda since she anticipated a busy afternoon back at the office.

"I don't want to pry," she murmured. At Elizabeth's slightly skeptical look, she insisted, "I really mean it. My dealings with David have to be strictly business."

"Oh, my, that sounds very dreary."

Jo had to agree, though not out loud. "Perhaps it does, but we both have responsibilities."

"No job is so important that it can be allowed to control your life. I'm sure even Jason, who is, after all, contending for the most important job of all, would be the first to tell you that."

"It's true he does put his family first...."

"Because he knows that in the long run that makes him a better, saner person and therefore potentially a better, saner president. Show me a man who cares for nothing but power, and I'll show you a very shallow and ultimately dangerous human being.

"When I was a girl," Elizabeth went on, "there was great stress placed on studying the classics. I remember being very impressed by the ancient Greek concept of the golden mean. All things in moderation; that's been the one basic rule of my life. I've tried to keep it in mind through the best of times and the worst."

"I know someone else who thinks that way," Jo said. "Perhaps you've met him. Francis MacInnes?"

It must have been her imagination, but she thought that Elizabeth paled slightly as she reached for a bread stick. "Ambassador MacInnes?"

"That's right. He was ambassador to Luxembourg, as well as doing a lot of other things in various governments. He's my landlord and, I'm glad to say, my friend."

"How nice.... It's been years since I last saw Francis. Fifteen or twenty, at least. He lost his wife some time ago, didn't he?"

Jo nodded. "I have the impression that it was quite rough on him, but he seems to have come out of it now."

"He was always a resilient man."

Apparently Elizabeth had known Francis better than she had first let on. Jo pondered that silently as she observed her hostess. Though she was in her mid-sixties, Elizabeth Stewart still had to be considered a beautiful woman. She had what the French so aptly referred to as good bones, which no amount of years could ever change.

Added to that, she carried herself with regal dignity while managing to retain an aura of warmth and genuine friendliness. It was an irresistible combination. Jo found herself warming to the older woman even as she began to suspect her motives in inviting her to lunch.

"You were going to tell me about David," she said softly.

Elizabeth smiled. "But you didn't want to hear."

"I've changed my mind."

"Among a woman's very few prerogatives. Well then, where to begin. He isn't actually my nephew. I'm more of an honorary aunt, but that hardly matters given how I feel about him. Has he told you about the navy?''

Jo nodded. "Submarine duty in the Arctic Circle. I said it must have been dreary; he disagreed."

"I don't think David has ever found anything in his life to be dreary, which is rather remarkable, all things considered. He seems to have been born with an ability to see the best in life, even at the worst of times."

"But he's so cynical," Jo said, struggling to reconcile the two viewpoints.

"Only on the surface. Besides, it isn't really cynicism so much as a deep sense of commitment and caring. He believes that people are fundamentally good, and he gets angry when they refuse to live up to that in themselves."

"Yes," Jo said slowly, "I can understand that. He talks about the importance of truth. A true cynic wouldn't believe that there was such a thing, let alone that it mattered."

"It sounds as though he's told you a great deal."

Jo shook her head. "Not really. We've had little time to talk together."

"Surely that could change?"

"It could, but that doesn't mean it will. I understand what you meant about not allowing our jobs to control us, but you have to realize that, for both David and me, our jobs represent far more than merely our livelihoods. They enable us to work for what we believe in."

Elizabeth thought about that for a moment. Softly she said, "You have a problem."

Jo nodded reluctantly. "And so far, no solution."

"If you wouldn't mind a bit of advice, dear, I've come to the conclusion over the years that we make the best decisions when we follow our hearts. Once in my life I failed to do that, and I've regretted it ever since."

Jo waited, giving Elizabeth the chance to elaborate if she cared to, but instead the older woman smiled, took another sip of her drink and said, "But I was telling you about David. Let me see now, I met him for the first time when he was about seven years old and..."

Several hours later Jo returned to her office. She felt rather guilty about being away so long, but was nonetheless glad that she had done so. At any rate no crises had developed during her absence. It was, in fact, unusually quiet, probably because it was a Friday and everyone was anxious to get out of town. Shelley was shoving a fistful of papers into her briefcase and slipping on her jacket, at the same time.

"Caught me," she said with a grin as Jo walked in. "I'm heading for a couple of days at the beach. With any luck it'll rain the whole time, and I won't be able to do anything but sleep."

"Enjoy yourself," Jo said. "Heaven knows you've earned it, and it'll be ages before another break comes along."

"Harry called," Shelley said. Harry Morton was the manager of the Greeley campaign, a hardheaded, experienced behind-the-scenes man who had worked for Jason Greeley from the first day he decided to enter politics. "The senator is more or less on schedule. He's due back Monday morning when he wants to get cracking on that trade bill."

"It's ready now," Jo said. She glanced at her desk, the top of which was uncharacteristically bare. It struck her that all her hard work of the past few weeks had paid off. For a change she was actually ahead of herself. "So is everything else he'll need next week."

"Why don't you take a break yourself? As you said, we won't have another chance anytime soon."

The idea was tempting, but Jo had barely begun to consider it when she realized that she wasn't looking forward to a weekend with nothing to do. That was surprising since she had always enjoyed her own company. But now all she could think of was how much better it would have been if David had been there to share the time with her. She caught herself wishing that he hadn't left that morning with the senator.

Elizabeth was certainly right: she had a problem. "Maybe I'll spend the weekend lying down with a cold cloth on my head," she muttered. "Or better yet, pounding some sense into it."

Shelley cast her a telling look. "Take it from me, honey, that doesn't work."

Jo was afraid she was right. As she sat slumped at her desk, desultorily making a list of things she should take care of the following week, David was uppermost in her mind. She kept remembering what it felt like to lie against his body, to feel his arms around her and his mouth on hers.

The neatly ruled yellow paper of her legal pad blurred before the image of his dark, tantalizing eyes. She caught herself doodling the picture of a man who looked remarkably like him. With an impatient snort, she ripped the page off and tossed it in the wastebasket.

The phone rang. Jo picked it up, realizing from the silence in the outer office that she was the last one left. Barely had she identified herself when a deep, frantic male voice shouted, "It's the wrong one, for God's sake! He's got the wrong one!"

Jo took a deep breath and gripped the phone more tightly. At the best of times, Harry Morton tended to be on the volatile side. Under pressure he could spew shrapnel in all directions. "Take it easy, Harry. Just tell me, the wrong what?"

"Wrong speech! What didja think I was talking about? The foreign policy speech for the wingding tonight. We brought the wrong version."

Jo winced. She didn't have to be reminded that the earlier version of the speech hadn't been as well thought out as it should have been. That happened sometimes, particularly where complex issues were concerned. No harm was done so long as the mistakes were caught during a rewrite.

And that was exactly what had been done. The final version of the speech was perceptive, cogent and— if she did say so herself since she had had a hand in writing it—brilliant. The earlier version was anything but.

"Harry, he can't deliver what he's got."

"You're telling me? I haven't let on to him 'cause he's got enough on his mind, and who wants to make him madder than hell anyway. But we've got to have the right version before tomorrow evening. Look," he went on, having calmed down enough to start thinking about what should be done, "here's how we handle it. Round up some kid who'd like a free trip to New York—one of the pages would be a good bet—

give them the speech, some money, and stick them on the next shuttle. Okay?''

''Not okay. First, we don't want this to get out.''

''Jeez, I should have thought of that.''

''This is too important to trust to anyone else. I'll bring it myself.''

''You're a good egg, kid.''

''Fess up, Harry, that's what you expected me to say.''

''Well, maybe...''

Jo's amusement showed in her voice. She was smiling as she hung up the phone after assuring Harry that she would be in New York in a few hours. The campaign manager's clumsy efforts to get her to do what he wanted didn't offend her. When Harry wanted to be, he was right up there with the smoothest operators in Washington. She considered it a compliment that he didn't try to use his technique on her.

Besides, he had provided her with a way out of an otherwise boring weekend, not to mention an excuse to see David. Not to mention it at all, since she wasn't about to admit he had slipped into her mind the moment she thought of taking the speech herself.

It took her little more than an hour to get home, pack a bag and turn Wilson over to Francis.

''I really appreciate your looking after him,'' she said as she deposited the kitten in her landlord's capable hands.

''My pleasure,'' he assured her. Wilson purred his accord.

''Ungrateful beast,'' Jo said. ''He's already forgotten me.''

''Nonsense, he's merely making the best of it.''

Jo didn't believe that for a moment, but she gave the kitten an affectionate pat before heading for the airport. Traffic was backed up even more than usual, and Jo barely made the 6:00 p.m. shuttle to New York. She darted on board just before the doors closed and took her seat as the plane was pulling away from the terminal.

As usual the flight was crowded. Lawyers, lobbyists and assorted other businesspeople who frequented the capital during the week rarely stayed around once the weekend came, but that didn't mean they were averse to working on the way home.

Barely had Jo settled in beside a tanned, gray-suited man in his mid-thirties than he gave her a toothy smile and said, "Say, aren't you Senator Greeley's aide?"

Jo smothered a sigh as she nodded. The man looked vaguely familiar, so she supposed she had met him at one of the innumerable Washington functions she had to frequent. Clearly he meant to make the most of her captive presence at his side for the next hour or so.

In the back of her mind, Jo felt a twinge of amusement at her own irritation. The man was undeniably handsome in a male model sort of way. He could have stepped intact from the pages of *Gentlemen's Quarterly*. She should have been impressed, but instead all she could really think of was David and how much she was looking forward to seeing him.

She tried to deny that to herself, but her natural caution and her best resolves were fast eroding. Somewhat weakly she told herself that it couldn't do any harm to merely be in the same room with him again. Surely they could be cordial to each other while keeping their distance.

The man next to her—Jo never did make note of his name—did his best to interest her in whatever it was he was supporting. She had the vague impression that it had something to do with tax cuts for the oil industry, but she paid little attention to what he was saying. She did, however, appear to listen with apparent politeness, though she turned down both his offer to buy her a drink and his suggestion that they have dinner together.

Barely had the plane reached the terminal at New York's LaGuardia Airport than Jo was on her feet. For once, arrival was on time. Luck continued to be with her as she snagged a cab immediately.

For his campaign trips to New York, Senator Greeley favored a relatively small, highly discreet hotel on the Upper East Side. He would have preferred to stay at his home out on Long Island, but time and logistics generally made that impossible.

As Jo hurried through the lobby, she took note of the several Secret Service agents who were maintaining a quiet presence near the doors and elevators. They would monitor everyone who entered or left, looking for anything that might arouse suspicion.

Jo had to show her identification before she was allowed onto the only elevator that could reach the floor where the senator and his staff were housed. As she stepped off, Harry Morton was there to greet her. The portly, disheveled man wasted no time in greetings. He took one look at Jo and held out a pudgy hand. "I was starting to get nervous. Give 'em here."

Jo extracted the papers from her briefcase, turned them over and was rewarded with a smile from Harry.

"You get a gold star for this, sweetie. Now could you do one other thing for me?"

"Sure, honey cakes, name it."

Harry sighed and rolled his eyes. "I did it again, didn't I? Forgot you don't like me calling you sweetie. I don't mean to be patronizing, honest. It just comes naturally."

"I believe you, Harry. It's not a big deal."

"You think I'm a throwback to the days before women's lib."

"Aren't you?" she asked with a smile.

"Well, yeah, but . . ."

"It's okay, Harry. You can be yourself with me, at least so long as you keep winning elections."

He gave her a grin and waved the papers. "We're gonna win this one, sweetie. I can smell it coming."

Jo believed him. There was an energy about the men and women hurrying back and forth along the corridor that bespoke tremendous confidence and commitment. No one seeing them could believe that they would not succeed. But more than that, Jo was convinced that they deserved to be victorious because of what they and their candidate stood for.

Which was a laudable sentiment but did not, as her mother always said, get the potatoes peeled. So long as she was in New York, Jo intended to make herself useful, beginning with Harry, who upon closer examination didn't seem to be bearing up as well as usual.

"Something wrong?" she asked.

His dour face arranged itself into even more somber lines. "How much time do we have? You want to hear about the screwed-up campaign flyers, the TV spot that's ten seconds too long or the latest bit of cheery news, which is that we may not be able to get out of here tonight 'cause of an airline strike.''

"What strike? I didn't hear anything about that.''

"It's a wildcat action. Something to do with rumors about another takeover that would eliminate jobs. We're okay so long as it's the flight attendants and pilots, since the senator charters his own plane. But if the mechanics go, we're stuck.''

"I don't think I can help you with that one, Harry.''

He sighed deeply and took a swipe at his forehead with a crumpled handkerchief. "But there is a little item you could help with. In my worst nightmares—and I mean my *worst*—I didn't imagine getting David Wilson dropped on me.''

Jo bit her lower lip, afraid of what was coming. "You heard about that?''

"Heard about it? I walked straight into it. Would it have been too much trouble for somebody to tell me that Attila the Hun was going to be dogging our candidate's heels?''

"He's really not that bad, Harry.''

"He who? Attila? Maybe I'm ruining his reputation by comparing him to David Wilson. All I know is the senator's in there right now—'' he tilted his head in the direction of Jason's suite "—having a chat with him, and the longer it goes on, the more my stomach feels like a July Fourth fireworks display is going off inside it. You get what I mean?''

"You're worried the senator will say something wrong?''

"Smart girl. But that's the least of it. He can toe the line one hundred percent, not make a single slip and still who knows what Wilson will do to him. He shreds people like we shred paper."

"Do you really do that?" Jo asked, curious despite herself.

Harry rolled his bloodshot eyes. "It's just an expression. For God's sake, don't use it around Wilson. Just do me a favor and go in there, make nice and tell the senator he's got to get a move on."

"Why don't you do it?"

"Because I'm not a good-looking dame. Wilson'll ignore me and stick with Greeley like glue."

"You're not seriously suggesting that I—"

"Use your feminine wiles? Sure, I am. What else have you got them for?"

"Harry, sometimes you really go too far."

Despite her stern words, he sensed capitulation in her tone and grinned unrepentantly. "Good thing I'm cute then, huh? So how about it?"

"Well..." Jo glanced at her watch as she remembered the evening's schedule. "It's true the senator is going to be running late soon."

"Good girl, I knew I could count on you."

Jo smothered a sigh. She started toward the senator's suite, paused, and looked back at the campaign manager. "You know, Harry, there aren't too many guys like you left. Maybe you should push for some kind of preservation effort. Save The Chauvinist. Kind of catchy, don't you think?"

"Beats those damn whales," he muttered and took himself off, leaving her to deal with the senator—and David.

## Chapter 7

Nice interference play," David said lightly as the door closed behind the departing senator. "But then you did have the element of surprise on your side."

Jo tossed her briefcase into a nearby chair and shot him a quick glance. Quick, because she had the definite impression that if she let herself look at him too closely, she would go on doing exactly that to the exclusion of all else.

The man had a nerve, looking that good after a hard day in pursuit of the news. His gray pinstripe suit was quietly elegant while his slightly undone tie and faint five o'clock shadow added a note of rakish masculinity. Added to all that was the smile playing about his firm mouth, which did nothing whatsoever for her equilibrium.

"We had a problem," she said as she turned her back to pour herself a glass of club soda from the bar. "I had to come."

"I'm not complaining."

She took a sip of the soda and looked at him again. He was sitting comfortably slouched on the couch with his arms resting on the back of it, and his long legs stretched out in front. If he was at all tense about her being there, he certainly didn't show it.

"How did your talk with the senator go?" she asked, seeking a safe topic.

David frowned. "I know you're supposed to be riding shotgun for him, but I draw the line at telling you what we discussed. If you want to know that, ask him."

"I'm not trying to check up on you," she said, angry that he had misinterpreted her innocent question. Or had it been so innocent? The fact was that she did have some of the same concerns as Harry Morton. But she also trusted Jason to handle himself well in any situation.

"I've decided that what you make of this story is your own business, and I can't worry about it. All I meant was that if there are points you want clarified, I might be able to help."

"Thanks, but I'll do my own clarifying."

"Then there is something...?"

His mouth tightened. "Let it go, Jo. This is tough enough for both of us without you trying to protect Greeley from me."

A rush of heat reddened Jo's face. She rarely had much of a temper, but David had a real knack for making her act out of character. "You've got a nerve," she said, "telling me how tough it is. You think I like the way things are? I didn't ask to be attracted to you, you know. I've got more than enough on my plate without adding you, too."

"That cuts both ways," David snapped. "The last thing I needed was a conflict like this in my life. If I had any sense, I'd steer as far away from you as I possibly could."

"Fine with me," Jo shot back. "I'll tell the senator we can't get along and ask him to assign someone else to work with you."

"You'd do that?"

"I..." Jo hesitated. Much as she hated to admit it, she loathed the idea of asking for a replacement. Besides the fact that it smacked of self-defeat, she knew that Greeley would insist on an explanation that would deeply embarrass her. Slowly she said, "There's really no point."

"Good, because I've got to tell you, if Greeley put somebody like that Morton character onto me, there'd be hell to pay."

Despite herself, Jo grinned. "Don't tell me you and Harry haven't hit it off?"

"Oh, I respect the man, all right. He's got a great track record, but he didn't exactly get it by being open and aboveboard."

"He runs an honest campaign," Jo insisted. "The senator makes sure of that."

"So far as he can, but you can't convince me that Greeley knows every single thing that goes on around him."

"Of course not, but he sets the standard, and everyone who works for him knows that they either live up to it or get out. Harry's no exception."

"Let's not argue about it," David said, surprising her since she was getting the definite impression that he relished few things as much as a good argument. "Why don't you sit down and relax for a while?"

"I should go over to where the senator's speaking and help out."

"Will the world end if you don't?"

"Probably not," she admitted with a slight smile as she sat down next to him. After the hectic plane ride and the dash to the hotel, it did feel good to rest for a few minutes. They sat in companionable silence until she said, "By the way, I had lunch with Elizabeth today."

David closed his eyes for a moment and laughed. "I might have known. She doesn't miss a trick."

"She's also very forthright. It seems I owe you an apology, by the way, for presuming that you talked her into bringing you to the dinner. She says it was her idea."

"Elizabeth," he said flatly, "has plenty of those. Be warned."

"I . . . uh . . . hesitate to mention it, but she seems to have at least one about us."

"It's the romantic in her. She's been wanting to see me settled down for years."

"I don't blame her," Jo said softly. "A little family life wouldn't do you any harm."

Behind his sardonic smile there was defensiveness. "Is that an offer?"

She flushed and looked away. "Of course not. I only meant—"

"Don't feel sorry for me, Jo," he broke in. "Whatever gory details Elizabeth told you, and I get the feeling there were plenty, I've managed just fine."

"I wasn't suggesting otherwise. Besides, she didn't say very much. I just got the impression that you hadn't had it easy, that's all."

David shrugged lightly and reached for the beer on the table in front of him. He took a long swallow, the muscles of his throat working, before he said, "Lots of kids grow up with lousy parents and still manage to survive. Mine were young, foolish and just plain unlucky."

"What happened to them?"

"They were killed when I was eight. Coming home from a party, they slammed head-on into a truck. If they'd been a little bit better parents, I would have been with them instead of having been left behind at the party."

"They forgot about you?" Jo asked, unable to hide her dismay.

"I was asleep in the closet. They forgot their coats, too." At the look on her face, he said gently, "Look, it was a long time ago, and everything worked out fine in the end. I spent some time in an orphanage, which was not as bad as you probably think, and then I joined the navy."

"How did you meet Elizabeth?"

He laughed softly. "She was Lady Bountiful. Every week or so, she'd visit the orphanage, bring presents for the kids, take some of us out for excursions. Of course, we all fantasized about being adopted by her, but that never happened."

"Why not? If she cared so much about children...?"

"Her husband wouldn't hear of it. From what I gathered afterward, he was determined that if they couldn't have kids for themselves, they'd remain childless. Nice guy."

"She could have left him."

"Her family was very conservative. They'd raised her to believe that divorce was shameful. Besides, if she had left she still wouldn't have been able to adopt any of us. Single women weren't permitted to do that back then."

"What a shame," Jo murmured, "for you and for Elizabeth. She could have done so much."

"Actually, she did a great deal. Just knowing that someone cared about me kept me from going completely over the edge."

Jo thought of the little boy he had been, lost and alone, and swallowed hastily. Her emotions were perilously close to the surface. The last thing she wanted to do was make a fool of herself.

His eyes lightened as he watched her. Slowly he reached over and traced a finger down her cheek. "You care about children."

It wasn't a question, but she nodded anyway. "Most people do."

"In a superficial way, but not enough to feel their helplessness and their need." Without warning, he asked, "Are you going to have children?"

"I don't know...I hope..."

"If the right man comes along?"

"Yes, I suppose that's it."

He said nothing more, but in the silence that followed she felt him looking, not at her, but into her as though he could see past the barriers of skin and bone to her very soul. The sensation would have disturbed her except that it was mutual.

Studying him, it was as though she could see, all at the same time, the man he was, the child he had been, the man he would become. A great tenderness welled within her. She wanted nothing so much as to reach out to him, to share with him her passion and her gentleness, to soothe away the cares of the world and be a sanctuary against pain and despair for him.

What she yearned for was written in her eyes. He sighed deeply and drew her close. "Talk to me, Jo. Tell me a story to keep me from thinking about how beautiful and desirable you are."

She smiled against the crisp wool of his suit jacket imbued with the scent of his woodsy after-shave. "You're the storyteller."

"I've told mine. It's your turn."

"There isn't much to it. You already know that I grew up on a ranch."

"With horses, right?"

"Some, for getting around on. But we raised cattle. Lots and lots of the great, smelly, bawling beasts. My earliest memory is of watching the spring branding. I can still smell the burned hides and hear the shouts of the men mingling with the animals' cries."

"That isn't exactly the romantic image I had in mind," he said slowly. "I thought you'd tell me how much you loved the place, how great it was, that sort of thing."

"If I'd loved it, I would have married Robbie Bender when I was eighteen and settled down to raise little Robbies."

"Who was Robbie Bender?" David asked none too lightly.

"My high school sweetheart. His family owned— still owns—the next ranch over. The Benders all figured me for their future daughter-in-law."

"Is that what your family expected, too?"

Jo shook her head. "I think they sort of hoped, but they knew deep down inside that I didn't belong there. I had to leave to find my proper place."

"And have you?"

She sat up and brushed a stray curl of hair back from her forehead. Her gray eyes were wide with candor as she said, "Up to a point. Until a short time ago, I found my life very satisfying."

"And now?"

"You know the answer to that, David. Just as you know that we're going 'round and 'round in circles. We both admit to desiring each other, we're both afraid of the complications that creates, we both think we should be able to keep each other at arm's length, but I think we both admit that it isn't working."

He smiled faintly, though the lines around his mouth deepened with wariness. "As neat a summary as I could have asked for. Do you also have a solution?"

"I'm not sure...."

"But you've got something in mind. What is it?"

She was very tempted to blurt out what she'd been thinking, but a modicum of self-preservation stopped her. Instead she rose, smoothed her skirt with unsteady hands and said, "I really should go over to the rally."

David remained seated. He looked at her with a faint hint of mockery. "Go ahead if that will make you feel safer."

"That's not the reason."

"Then what is?"

"I . . . I can be impulsive sometimes. I'm trying not to be in this case."

"Some of the greatest moments in my life have come from impulses."

"I'm sure," she said sardonically, "but I'd rather not be party to another one."

"You're admitting that it would be great?"

"I don't believe I've ever denied it. Obviously the chemistry between us is . . . unusual."

He gave a short laugh as he stood up. "I could think of a few other words to describe it."

"Yes . . . well, words are your business." She took several steps backward as she glanced around nervously, looking for her briefcase. She had rarely felt so out of her depth. She wanted to run, but whether to David or from him she couldn't be sure. Escape seemed the more prudent course, if only because it bought her more time.

"I'll . . . uh . . . see you later, I guess," she murmured.

He straightened his tie and looked at her steadily. "You can count on it."

It was exactly what she had been doing, Jo realized a few hours later when she returned to the hotel to find David absent. Harry's worst fears had come true. The airport mechanics had gone on strike, and the only planes that were taking off were charters maintained by strikebreakers. A presidential candidate could hardly go that route, so the senator and the entire Greeley campaign were stuck in New York at least until the following morning.

That didn't bother Jason at all. "Let me know when you get this straightened out," he told his perspiring campaign manager with a grin as he headed off to get something to eat.

"I swear he doesn't care," Harry muttered as the elevator doors closed and the senator disappeared from sight. "Worse thing in the world that can happen at this stage is for the candidate to get cocky. He's acting like he's already got it won when it's anything but."

"He doesn't think that," Jo corrected quietly. "He's just glad of the break. You can't blame him for that."

"Wanna bet?" Harry growled. "He can put his feet up all he wants once he's in the Oval Office, but before then he's got to keep them smack on the ground."

"You don't really believe that running for president is harder than actually serving in the office?" Jo challenged as they walked down the corridor toward the room set aside as a hospitality suite for campaign workers and chosen others. Hot coffee, cold drinks and food were available there at all hours. Since neither Harry nor Jo had gotten a chance to eat during the rally, they were grateful for the nourishment.

"All I know," Harry said as he picked up a paper plate and began piling it high with sandwiches, "is that it's the winning that counts. Jason had damn well better remember that."

Jo helped herself to a few spoonfuls of shrimp salad that looked reasonably fresh, added a handful of crackers and picked up a can of diet soda. So much for gourmet dining. "He wants to spend a night with his wife in their home. Is that really such a problem?"

Harry shrugged. "At least he isn't into broads. Jeez, I could tell you stories...." He flopped down on the couch in front of the television and flipped the remote control.

The head and shoulders of a lovely young woman with honey-colored hair came into view. She sat at a desk in front of a plain blue backdrop. The mauve silk suit she wore was elegant yet feminine. She looked directly into the camera, her eyes alive with intelligence and vitality. "That's the latest on the international front," Judith Fairchild said. "We'll be right back after a word from our sponsor."

"They're everywhere these days," Harry grumbled as he took an oversize bite from one of the sandwiches on his plate.

"Commercials?" Jo asked as she sat down.

"No, women." His mouth was full, but he still managed to get the words out. "Now they're even anchoring the nightly news."

"Poor Harry, next thing you know, we'll want the vote."

"That was our big mistake," he said. "Ever since women got emancipated, we've had to bend over backward to keep from offending them. Used to be a guy could slip a few times, other guys understood. But now if you want to get elected to anything, you've got to be purer than the driven snow."

"Then you ought to thank us for holding our nation's leaders to a higher standard of behavior."

"You would look at it that way."

Jo laughed. At a younger, more sensitive age, she would have been offended by Harry's mistrust of women. But time had taught her a thing or two. She knew he had the same worries as a lot of men—whether women would displace them in their traditional occupations, if women would still be on hand to give the support and encouragement men were accustomed to, even if women would continue to need men once they achieved financial independence.

For herself, she chose to believe that men and women did best together when they dealt as equals. That didn't mean there were no differences between them, far from it. But then she would be the first to admit that it was the differences that made life interesting.

The commercials ended, and Judith Fairchild came back on the screen. "And now, let's go to our political commentator, David Wilson, who's in New York this evening. David, the presidential campaign is swinging into high gear now. The early primaries show Jason Greeley as the favorite. Do you think he's got the nomination locked up?"

Jo held her breath as the camera switched to David. He was wearing the same suit and tie and his hair was neatly combed, but he hadn't shaved. The faint five o'clock shadow gave him a rough-edged air that was a sharp contrast to the usual bland personalities that showed up on the television screen.

"I wouldn't say that, Judith," David answered cordially. "We've got several months yet to the convention, and a great deal could still happen. It's true that Jason Greeley is definitely the front-runner, but all that really means is that his candidacy is coming under the closest scrutiny ever. He's created a very high level of expectation in the minds of potential voters. If he slips, even mildly, they're going to be disillusioned."

"You sound as though you think there may be trouble ahead for the senator," Judith said.

"I'm saying he's going to be under enormous pressure, and we're going to find out whether or not he can take it."

"There are those who believe that our system for electing a president is too harsh, that it discourages the best people from running. Care to comment on that?"

David shrugged. "It's true nobody makes it to the White House these days without running a very tough gauntlet. People with problems they would rather not have aired in public are choosing not to run, and that may be unfortunate because some of them are very qualified. But the fact remains that we can't afford to elect anyone we don't know for sure can stand up under enormous pressure. The last thing we need is a president who can't stay in control."

"What was it Harry Truman said?" Judith asked. "If you can't take the heat, stay out of the kitchen."

"That's it exactly. We have to know that Greeley, and anyone else who wants to be president, can take it once the going gets rough. We have to know how these people behave when there's a great deal at stake because, in the final analysis, we're entrusting our lives to whoever we elect."

"Food for thought," Judith said as she turned back to the audience. "David Wilson is preparing a special report on Jason Greeley and his candidacy. We'll look forward to seeing it soon. In the meantime, that's it for tonight."

As the news ended and another batch of commercials came on, Harry put down his plate and said quietly, "We're in trouble."

"What are you talking about?"

"Wilson, he's got something."

"What did he say that makes you think that?" Jo asked, bewildered. She had been so caught up in watching David that she was barely aware of what he had said, but surely she hadn't missed anything cataclysmic.

"That bit about the senator not having the nomination locked up yet."

"But it's true, he doesn't."

"That isn't the point. Add it to what he said about disillusioning the voters, taking the heat, all that stuff. He's on to something."

"I don't understand," Jo said. "Even if you're right, what could it be?"

Harry shot her a sharp look. "How would I know? It's Wilson who's got the info." He jumped up and began pacing back and forth. His eyes narrowed as he surveyed her thoughtfully. "And you're the one who can get it from him."

Jo stiffened. "Stop right there, Harry. I was happy enough to run interference for you this evening, but that's where I draw the line. There is absolutely no way that I'm going to try to find out what, if anything, David is working on."

"Not even if you'd be doing him a favor?"

"What do you mean?"

"Just that whatever he thinks he's got, he's wrong. Take it from me, this campaign is so squeaky clean it hurts. If Wilson believes otherwise, he's riding for a nasty fall."

"Then he'll just have to take the risk," Jo said, with more conviction than she actually felt. The thought that David might be following a lead that would result in his embarrassment worried her deeply. But there was nothing she could do about it. Or so she told herself.

# Chapter 8

There was also nothing she could do about the mechanics' strike that shut down the New York airports that night. Had Jason Greeley been other than who and what he was—say an industrial tycoon, a rock star, an eccentric millionaire—he could have hired scab mechanics and flown out of town right on schedule. But there was absolutely no way a candidate for the presidency could break a picket line. Greeley said as much when he philosophically accepted the predicament.

"Boss," Harry growled, "we've got a swing through New England starting tomorrow. Remember, New Hampshire, all those folks who voted for you in the primary? Connecticut, Maine, Massachusetts. They've got voters there, too, you know. Voters who expect to see you."

Despite the late hour—by then it was close to one in the morning—Jason smiled. He pretended to give the matter close consideration, then asked, "Exactly how many voters, Harry? After all, what's another million or so?"

"He's kidding," Harry yelled in the direction of David, who was standing off to one side taking the whole thing in. "Great sense of humor, this guy. But seriously, boss, what're we gonna do?"

"We're gonna get in our cars and drive, Harry," the candidate said in an exact parody of his campaign manager's tone. More seriously, he added, "We can spend the night in Stamford and go on to New Haven in the morning in plenty of time for my first appearance."

"Stamford?" Harry repeated doubtfully.

"Connecticut," Jason explained. "It's right over the border from Westchester County. Get us some hotel rooms lined up, and we'll be all set."

"They got hotels there?"

"Harry, your parochialism is showing and in front of David Wilson, no less."

"Just kidding, boss. Stamford, hotels, get on it right away."

He bustled off, returning a few moments later to announce that everything was taken care of, and they could get started immediately. In fact only a few of them could since there was a shortage of cars.

The Secret Service had plenty, but they wouldn't let anyone ride with them. They were not at all happy about the sudden change of plans since it left them with no time to clear the senator's route. They had to settle for putting two cars in front of him and two behind and hoping that would be enough.

Harry had managed to scare up three rentals. He insisted on driving one of them and, being a notorious incompetent behind the wheel, found himself hard-pressed for passengers. Jo and David crowded into a car driven by one of Harry's long-suffering assistants.

Squeezed into the back seat as they were, it was all but impossible to remain unaware of each other. They tried talking, but were both too worn out for that. At length, Jo fell asleep, her head on David's shoulder and his arm around her.

She awoke, startled to find herself in that position, as they drove into the hotel parking lot. David helped her out of the car, but held himself aloof as they went through the formalities at the desk and were finally given their keys.

Jason rode up in a separate elevator surrounded by nervous agents. Jo and the rest followed. The short notice given to the hotel had left the entourage scattered over several floors, so she was surprised to discover that she and David had been given adjacent rooms. But no more surprised than he.

Despite the fatigue and the wariness they both shared, she returned his ironic smile as he said, "This is going to go down in my book as one of the great wasted opportunities of my life."

She unlocked her door and opened it. "I could make some remark about what makes you think there was even an opportunity, or, if there was one, why waste it. But we're both too pooped for that, so all I'm going to say is good night."

"Sensible woman," he murmured as he stepped inside his own room and firmly, if reluctantly, closed the door.

She could hear him moving around even as she was and tried very hard not to think about him getting ready for bed. Fortunately she really was exhausted and fell asleep almost the instant her head hit the pillow, only to wake scant hours later to the shrill ring of the phone beside the bed.

With a low moan she rolled out from beneath the covers and stumbled into the bathroom. A shower was going on the other side. She turned the water on in hers, stripped off her nightgown and without bothering to test the temperature, stepped under the nozzle.

"Aaagh!"

There was silence on the other side of the wall for a moment, then, "Jo? Are you all right?"

She hopped back out from under the shower and stood beside it shivering and cursing as she turned the water from cold to warm. "Yes," she called, "I'm okay."

"Sure?"

"Yes," she insisted more firmly. "I just hate waking up like this."

David laughed. "I know what you mean." He turned his shower back on as she gingerly stuck a hand under hers to make sure it was safe. Only then did she step into the cubicle again. As she put soap on a washcloth and began running it over herself, it occurred to her that David was doing much the same a scant few inches away.

A wave of heat that had nothing to do with the temperature of the water struck her. She closed her eyes against the image of his body, naked and slick, so near to her own. Her nipples hardened, and she swayed against the wall of the shower.

A soft groan, more of astonishment than arousal, broke from her. She was amazed by her response at the mere thought of him. Nothing of that sort had ever happened to her before. At a loss as to how to deal with it, she had no choice but to simply wait until the wave of heat subsided enough for her to finish the shower and get out.

Deliberately keeping her mind blank, she toweled herself dry and went hurriedly through the motions of dressing. Her eyes still held a distant and preoccupied look when she emerged from her room a few minutes later, in time to encounter David in the hallway.

It registered with her that he looked similarly distracted, but she had no opportunity to wonder why as he asked, "Sleep well?"

"Like a log. You?"

"Great, though not long enough. It's been a while since I followed a campaign full-time. I'd forgotten what a grind it is."

"The mind has a way of mercifully blanking out memories like that," she said as they walked together toward the elevator. They got in, and David pushed the button for the main floor.

"Have you had breakfast yet?"

Jo shook her head. "No, I was going to grab a bite and then check in with the senator."

"Mind if I join you?"

"Of course not." Besides the fact that it would be obviously rude to decline his company, she couldn't deny that she relished the thought of some time alone

with him. Or as alone as anyone could be in a bus-
tling hotel restaurant.

A crowd of blurry-eyed guests, many of whom were
with the campaign, sat ensconced at the tables and
counter. Several looked up and nodded as Jo came in.
She returned the greetings, but was glad when no one
suggested that she and David join them. It was automatically presumed that they were going to discuss
business and preferred to do so alone.

Actually there was nothing Jo wanted to talk about
less. As a result, she was disconcerted when, after they
had given their orders, David said, "There's a new poll
out. Greeley's climbed a couple of points."

She sighed inwardly and managed to shift gears
without too much visible effort. "He has momen-
tum."

"Today, but he's going to have a fight to hold on to
it."

She shrugged and took a sip of the orange juice the
waitress had set in front of her. It wasn't fresh and had
a metallic taste that made her grimace. She set it down
again and reached for the coffee instead. "Why is it,"
she asked a moment later, "that places like this never
have decent coffee?"

"They skimp on how much they use and hope no
one will notice. Try tea instead." He took a look in the
pot the waitress had put before him, decided to let it
brew a while longer and returned his attention to her.
"You look lovely this morning, but then you always
do."

Shifting gears again. The man was definitely keeping her off balance. She concentrated on buttering her
toast. "Thank you."

He smiled. "Another thing, you're always so polite."

"Is there something wrong with that?"

"No, of course not. It's just that when a man tells a woman he thinks she's lovely and she says thank you, in that slightly cautious tone, I want to know what she's thinking. Is she wondering whether the man meant what he said, whether she's pleased or not or whether she wants him to go further?"

"Probably all of the above," Jo said with a smile. She wasn't used to hearing a man express such candid interest in a woman's thoughts, and it took a little getting used to. In her experience, men as attractive as David simply presumed that any woman was flattered by their approval and their advances. He presumed nothing, but then she was coming to understand that he never did.

"Right now," she said honestly, "I'm thinking about being here with you, but I'm also thinking about the hundred or so things I'll probably have to do today. I'm wondering about how the senator is holding up, about whether Harry Morton and I are destined to some day come to blows and about when the airline strike will end."

She broke off as the waitress placed their eggs in front of them. Halfheartedly she murmured, "I asked for scrambled."

The waitress paused in the act of gazing admiringly at David and deigned to glance at her plate. "Those are fried."

"Right, not scrambled."

"Oh..."

Jo suppressed a sigh. She could have insisted that the woman take her order back, but the waitress looked tired even at that early hour. She had brightened at the sight of David, but there was no denying her underlying weariness. Jo glanced at the chapped hands that had held their plates and noticed the thin gold wedding band that was scratched in several places. On the other hand was a high-school-class ring, also scratched from rough years of wear.

Quietly she said, "Never mind about the eggs, they're fine. Tell me, do you live around here?"

The waitress raised her eyebrows. "Are you kidding? Who can afford the rents? And just try to buy a place. Everything's out of sight."

"Then you must commute."

The woman nodded. She was surprised by Jo's interest, but not turned off by it. Instead she bent her hip slightly to rest her weight and said, "From Bridgeport, on the train. It's not too bad, just takes a while. Of course, the same thing's starting to happen there so who knows how long we'll be able to stay."

"What about your kids?" Jo asked. "Do you have any?"

"Two, a boy and a girl in junior high. I've gotta admit I worry about them. I'd like to be home when they get out of school, but there's just no way."

"It must be tough," Jo said softly.

The waitress shrugged. She straightened up again as the table nearby began to fill up. "It's life. Not enough money, nobody home with the children and no place decent to live. Been like that for a while now so we ought to be getting used to it. Only thing is," she added softly, "I wonder what to tell my kids. They want to know why, hard as me and their father work, we can't live better than we do."

"What do you tell them?" David asked quietly.

The woman smiled ruefully. "I tell them they'll have an easier time of it if they really study hard. There are opportunities in computers and stuff like that. But their father and me never learned anything about that, and now it seems like it's too late for us. 'Course, I'm not sure how much they're learning, either."

"The schools need more money if they're going to do the job for the next generation," Jo said when the woman had gone on to the next table. "And older people like that need to have retraining available to them. The jobs they were trained for are disappearing or are paying only a fraction of what they used to. It isn't right."

"You think money's the solution?" David asked.

"No, but it sure doesn't hurt. The point is we need somebody who will set policies that will help families, especially women and children who have borne the brunt of the economic dislocation that's occurred in the last few years."

"Greeley talks a lot about that," David acknowledged. "Do you think he means it?"

"Yes," Jo said simply. "If I didn't, I wouldn't be working for him."

They finished breakfast in silence, David mulling over what Jo had said while she wondered where his thoughts were taking him. Was Harry's speculation correct, did he really have something on Greeley? She couldn't imagine for a moment what that might be, but she was well aware that anyone's past could be made to look tarnished given sufficient effort. She had to count on David being too fair to do that.

The stopover in Stamford led to an impromptu tour of a senior citizens' center where the senator gave a brief talk about improving medical coverage, then mingled with the audience. He was well received, and Jo heard a number of the older men and women murmuring out of his earshot what a nice boy he was. She grinned at that, making a mental note to tell him what his image was with that particular group at least.

"What do they want?" Harry was muttering as they returned to their cars and the motorcade started up again. "Blood?"

"They who?" Jo asked. "Not those people in there?"

He waved a hand dismissively from the front seat where he was not, thankfully, driving. For once, he had been convinced to turn the wheel over to a sedate young aide who kept his eyes firmly on the road. "The mechanics. They're still out, and we're still grounded. It's like the Dark Ages, plodding from one place to another."

In the back seat, David and Jo exchanged a look. For once, traffic was flowing smoothly. They were making excellent time, but Harry wouldn't care about that. To him, a campaign was fought in an airplane as much as on the ground.

"Why don't you think about renting a train?" David asked. "Put Greeley out on a whistle-stop."

"You mean like Harry Truman?" Harry asked.

"Sure, why not?"

"That's kind of gimmicky, don't you think?" Jo interjected.

"What's wrong with gimmicks?" Harry promptly demanded. "They're the heart and soul of a campaign. How many original ideas do you think there are, anyway?" As though abruptly aware of who was listening to him, he added hastily, "Not that we need gimmicks, of course. Greeley's in solid."

David shrugged. "If you say so."

Harry lifted his shoulders and spread his hands. "It's not just me. The polls say so, the crowds say so, and let me tell you, the contributors say so. Off the record?"

"Sure," David agreed, "why not?"

"Just so we understand each other. Off the record, in the last two weeks this campaign took in over two million dollars in contributions. And that's with Greeley still refusing to take a dime from the special interest groups. Pretty impressive, huh?"

"Yes," David admitted, "it is. Where's the money coming from?"

"Some of it's from guys like the ones at that dinner the other night. But the thing that really gets to me is that most of it's from regular people. We're cashing a whole lot of checks for fifty bucks, a hundred. Doesn't sound like much, but believe me, it mounts up."

"I believe you," David said thoughtfully. "It is possible there's a ground swell underway for Greeley."

"Exactly how I'd put it," Harry said pointedly.

David gave him a chiding grin. "But we're off the record, right?"

"Well, hey, if you really want to use it . . ."

Jo shook her head ruefully. "Nice try, Harry, but I don't think it's going to fly."

The campaign manager attempted to look innocently baffled. "What do you mean? All I said was, if he wants to use it, it's okay."

"Ed Williams," David said, mentioning the name of a correspondent on another network, "is doing a piece on campaign financing. Why don't you tell him?"

"I was trying to give you a break," Harry claimed.

"Thanks," David said dryly. "But my story is on Greeley himself—the man, not the campaign. And no," he added quickly as Harry tried to interrupt, "they are not one and the same. There are plenty of people tagging along to report on where he went, what he said, things like that. I'm out for more."

"Yeah," Harry muttered as he turned back to stare out the front of the car, "I know you are."

Jo was silent. She, too, realized that David was looking for something far more substantial. The question was whether or not he would find it.

## Chapter 9

"You're wasted in Washington, kid," Harry said. "Your talent's on the road. You ought to be able to see that."

"Thanks," Jo muttered as she sucked on the tip of a finger. She had burned it that morning trying to smooth the wrinkles out of a skirt while using a borrowed iron and a towel spread out on a hotel bed. The skirt had fortunately come out better than she had. "But I prefer Washington. It's safer."

Harry started to laugh, ended up wheezing and took a drag on his cigarette. He kept meaning to quit, but was never in between campaigns long enough to accomplish it. "You might be right, though I never heard anybody say that before. Place is a snake pit, if you ask me."

"Then how come you want to work there?" she asked.

His unruly eyebrows rose almost to the level of his hairline. "Who said I did?"

"We all just presumed—"

"That I'm working for Greeley to get a cushy job in the White House? No way, sweetheart. Be like putting a fine stallion out to stud when he's still got plenty of wins left in him."

"Hold on to that thought, Harry," David advised with a grin. He was lying stretched out on the broken-down sofa that took up most of the small room where they were seated. Beyond the room was an auditorium where the senator was giving a speech. From the sounds that reached them, it was going well.

"Don't you think you ought to be out there?" Harry inquired, looking at him. "You know, soaking up atmosphere, picking up a few quotes, that sort of thing."

"Gee," David said innocently, "is that how it's done?"

"Don't pay any attention to him," Jo told Harry. "This is how he works."

The campaign manager took another look at the younger man and sighed theatrically. "Pretty nice work, if you ask me."

He stood up, made a halfhearted effort to tuck his shirt in and lumbered toward the door. "If you kids will excuse me, somebody has to make sure the wheels stay greased."

"Just kidding," Jo said automatically when he was gone. "I mean, he's not planning on bribing anyone or anything like that."

David shook his head chidingly. He thought she looked great sitting on a chair with her legs crossed and her skirt slightly hiked up. She had fabulous legs, not too much muscle, not too little. They went with the fabulous rest of her.

He closed his eyes for a moment, trying to get a grip on himself. He had it bad, all right, but that was no reason to act like an idiot. As coolly as he could manage, he said, "Such a suspicious mind. The thought would never have occurred to me."

Jo widened her gray eyes. "Really? I had the impression that was the kind of thing you loved."

David levered himself off the couch and came toward her. "You have all sorts of impressions. I'm not sure how many of them are well-founded."

She stiffened slightly, and her hand tightened on the sheaf of papers on her lap. "What do you mean?"

"Don't do that," he said.

"What?"

"Tense up like that. You do it every time I come near you. It's been going on for days, and it's driving me nuts."

"Is that why you've been such great company?"

It was his turn to be surprised. "What are you talking about?"

"Only that ever since we started on this little jaunt, we've been circling around each other like two caged dogs."

He frowned, and the corners of his mouth turned down. "Nice image. You might have tried for something more romantic."

"That's exactly what I'm trying to steer clear of."

"Which is the source of the problem. We're both trying too hard."

"It's been mutual, wouldn't you say?"

"Yes," he admitted with a heavy sigh, "but at least on my part, not terribly successful. I've still got the same problem I've had since the moment I walked into your office. You are too damned hard to be around, woman."

Jo gave him a long, steady look. "There's an obvious solution, you know."

He permitted himself a pleasantly lecherous grin. "Why is it that I suspect you aren't going to make the suggestion I'm hoping you'll make?"

"You could wrap up your story and leave."

"I was right. That wasn't the suggestion."

"Well, couldn't you?"

He shook his head and walked over to the soda machine. As he fished in his pockets for coins, he said, "I'm not done yet."

"You've been following the senator for almost a week now. How much more material do you need?"

"I'm not sure, but I'll know when I have it."

"Do you always work this way?"

He thought for a moment while he dropped a couple of quarters into the slot. "Yeah, I guess I do."

"Then you're lucky. Most people don't have the luxury of working without deadlines."

"Oh, I have a deadline. Or at least I did have. I've already missed it."

Jo couldn't quite contain her surprise. She'd had no idea of that. "Don't they mind at the network?"

"Sure they do. Especially since everyone's so cost conscious these days, the last thing they want is a correspondent who isn't coming through."

"David...I know it isn't really any of my business, but you aren't getting into some kind of trouble, are you?"

He took a swallow of his soda and shrugged. "What if I am? This is an important story. I'm going to do it right."

"That's very laudable, but—"

"You think I should go on the air without all the facts?"

"No, of course not, but..." She paused, presuming he was going to interrupt her again. When he didn't, she went on cautiously. "But we can't always do everything exactly the way we would like. Sometimes we have to compromise."

"Don't you think I know that? I've done my share of pleasing the powers that be, but I draw the line at sacrificing the integrity of a story to make the brass happy. This profile of Greeley will go on the air when it's ready, not before."

Jo took a deep breath. She needed to in order to hold back the question that was on the tip of her tongue. The more he talked, the more she wondered if perhaps Harry wasn't right. Integrity aside, David wasn't the kind of reporter who would hold up a story for one more detail, one more confirmation of a fact. If he was waiting, it had to be for something big.

Yet she could not bring herself to ask him. Mainly because if there was something, she didn't want to know.

They were on the road again within the hour. The senator made three more campaign stops that day before they finally stopped at a motel outside of Portland, Maine. It was raining again, but Jo was getting used to that. The spring had already been so rainy that she was surprised when the sun shone. This storm, however, was different. It whirled down out of Canada, struck the New England coast with a vengeance, and within a matter of hours flooded roads, blew down power lines and otherwise did its best to make everyone miserable.

Holed up in the motel, watching a stream wash by where the sidewalk usually was, the campaign came to a grinding halt. Like it or not, no one was going anywhere until the weather cleared.

"Get some rest," Jason directed the staff when he realized their predicament. "There's nothing else we can do."

Jo knew good advice when she heard it, but somehow she couldn't seem to comply. She went back to her room, lay down on her bed and listened to the rain drum against the roof. Always before, that sound had been guaranteed to put her to sleep; now it had no effect. The longer she stared at the ceiling, the more she thought about David.

The more she thought, the more she desired.

The more she desired, the more distant sleep became.

The more distant sleep became, the more imperative it was to do something, anything to distract herself.

With an exasperated groan, she got up, went into the bathroom and splashed cold water on her face. The eyes that looked back at her from the mirror were unnaturally bright. Their normally gray hue was darkened to a shade resembling the stormy sky. Her cheeks were slightly flushed and her lips, where she had bitten them while lying on the bed, were swollen.

She ran a brush through her tangled curls, refastened the belt around her lightweight knit dress and left the room. Outside, the corridor was empty except for the Secret Service agent on duty in front of Jason's suite. Jo gave him a smile as she passed by on her way downstairs.

She had barely stepped into the bar when she realized that most of the other campaign staffers were having no better luck resting than she. They had instinctively gathered together to have a few drinks, swap tall tales and generally keep the dismal day at bay.

Even the press was welcome. On even the most routine campaign appearances, Jason was automatically accompanied by several dozen reporters, photographers, cameramen and general hangers-on. No one interested in getting his message out to the public could object to such coverage, although everyone knew that it was really prompted by the possibility, however remote, that something newsworthy would occur at the least expected moment.

The candidate would make some tremendous gaffe that would expose his utter unsuitability for the office to which he aspired, or—and no one who had lived through the violence of recent decades could discount this possibility—something even worse would happen.

Harry was ensconced at the bar with a stein of beer and a bowl of peanuts in front of him. He was deep in conversation with several reporters, but looked up as she came in and waved. Jo waved back, but skirted the bar in favor of a table off to the side. She was hoping to find a few women friends and join them for a cosy chat. Instead, she found David.

He was seated alone at a table toward the back. Jo would have been willing to swear that she didn't know he was there when she headed in that direction, but she wondered if that was really true. He didn't ask her to sit, but merely rose when he saw her and held out a chair.

She took it without comment, smoothing her skirt over her knees as she did so. The gesture was a hold-over from the ladylike manners drilled into her in childhood and adolescence. Sometimes she seriously wondered if she might be the only woman who had grown up in the sixties and seventies who still remembered such niceties. Maybe not, since she seemed to remember reading just recently that white gloves had made a comeback.

When he sat down opposite her his face was slightly obscured by shadows. But she could still see that his dark blond hair was rumpled and his deep-set eyes were strained. Like her, he didn't appear to be sleeping very well. He was wearing a tan turtleneck under a tweed jacket that went well with his coloring, but could not completely banish the slightly haunted look around his eyes and mouth.

"What will you have?" he asked as the waiter noticed her and came over.

Jo ordered a sherry on the rocks with a twist of lime. She almost smiled at her choice, remembering how her mother had always told her that sherry was a safe drink to order on a date. That was because her mother had despised sherry and presumed that no one could drink enough of it to get into trouble. What she would have thought of it served over ice and gussied up with lime, Jo didn't know.

The silence between them persisted long enough to make her uncomfortable. She glanced at the television over the bar where a baseball game was in progress. Somewhere the sun was obviously shining. She wondered where as she said, "Think the Sox can do it this year?"

"I've got no idea," he said as he reached for a handful of peanuts and popped them into his mouth.

"You don't like baseball?"

He shook his head, swallowed and said, "It takes too long. Give me football anytime. Steelers versus anyone, that's my idea of a good afternoon."

Jo shrugged and accepted her sherry from the waiter. It had a chunk of lime instead of a twist, but she was used to that. Whichever she asked for, the opposite invariably came. "If you like to watch a bunch of thyroid cases mauling each other, football's fine. But for real sportsmanship, you have to go to baseball."

"You really like it that much?"

"I always have. You don't know what you're missing."

"A good snooze maybe. Baseball can put me to sleep, whereas football . . ."

They went on in that vein, debating the merits and demerits of their respective sports. The tension eased between them to be replaced by humor and the simple enjoyment of each other's company.

Yet beneath it all Jo couldn't shake the feeling that something was preying on David. She sensed a cer-

tain preoccupation in him that troubled her. Moreover she felt his eyes on her from time to time with a
brooding intensity she didn't normally associate with
him. It was on the tip of her tongue to ask him what
was wrong, but she hesitated, discouraged by the feeling she got that he wouldn't welcome any such inquiry.

There was a jukebox in the back of the bar. An old
sixties tune drifted out of it, and several couples got up
to dance.

"Come on," David said as he stood and held out his
hand.

Jo shrugged. Why not? It was raining outside, they
weren't going anywhere, and there was nothing else to
do.

He danced well, but then so did she. Nothing flashy,
just nice, slow swaying together as the music picked
them up and took them away. His body was hard
against her own, and he led easily, unobtrusively. She
rested her head on his shoulder and deliberately
stopped thinking.

When the song ended, another began. They kept
dancing. Jo was dimly aware of the other people
around them. Their voices made a faint background
hum that was in no way disturbing. Other couples
came and went on the small dance floor; they stayed.
It seemed right and very easy to merely drift with the
music. Jo's eyes were closed, her body relaxed, her
mouth curved in a slight smile. The hand that David
held nestled against his chest, and the other was behind his head. She felt his thick blond hair and her
smile deepened.

"You look very content," he murmured, his voice little more than a deep rumble beneath her cheek.

Her eyes shot open, meeting his. "I am," she said softly.

"You're sure that's a good idea?"

"No," she admitted, "not sure at all. Just not fighting it anymore."

"Why not?"

She thought for a moment, then shrugged. "I don't know. Instinct, I guess."

"Do you usually pay attention to that?"

"Oh, yes," she said. "Whenever I haven't, I've ended up regretting it."

They continued dancing. It was getting late, and the bar was emptying out. A waiter began moving around, putting the chairs up.

"I think they're trying to tell us something," David said quietly.

Jo glanced around and nodded with regret. "Looks that way."

They stepped apart, looking at each other. "That was very nice," David said.

"I thought so, too."

Moments passed while they stood unmoving, until a waiter stacking chairs looked at them and coughed.

"We'd better go," David said.

Jo nodded. They left the dance floor side by side but without touching. Neither spoke as the bar door closed behind them and they crossed the hotel lobby. A Secret Service man nodded as they stepped onto the elevator.

Their rooms were on the same floor though at opposite ends of the hallway. "I'll walk you to your door," David said.

Jo didn't object. The silence between them continued, lengthened. Her fingers were very stiff when she reached into her purse for her key. She had trouble holding on to it and fumbled as she tried to unlock the door.

"Let me," David said. He took the key from her. A moment later the lock clicked, and he pushed the door open. "Jo..."

Gray eyes met brown. She saw the passion in his, and the tenderness. All that and a question as well. Her throat tightened. She hovered for an instant on the edge of indecision, then instinct won, and she held out her hand.

## Chapter 10

Y ou are," David murmured as he eased the straps of the camisole from Jo's shoulders, "extraordinarily beautiful."

Her hands spread out beneath his opened shirt, her slender fingers pale against his sun-warmed skin. His chest was perfectly smooth like that of an ancient Greek statue, the kind she had stared at abashed but fascinated on grade school trips to the art museum. How much greater the fascination when such male perfection was viewed in flesh instead of stone.

His warm, lightly moist lips followed the path of the camisole's strap down her shoulder to the bend of her arm. She gasped softly as he nibbled at the soft inner skin. Tremors raced through her, making her sway weakly against him.

"You..." she murmured, stumbling, at a loss for words. "You..."

He raised his head, eyes gently mocking. "Yes?"

"You overwhelm me."

Her honesty was returned by genuine surprise. "I would have said it was the other way around."

She shook her head so that her short curls trembled slightly. "I don't understand."

"No," he said with a faintly bemused air, "I suppose you don't, but it doesn't matter." His hand cupped her shoulder as he slowly slid the other strap down. The camisole caught on the full curve of her breasts just above her nipples. She wasn't wearing a bra, having found the absence of a need for one to be a compensation for breasts which she had once considered too small. That concern no longer troubled her; she had matured beyond it. But even if she hadn't, David's obvious appreciation would have reassured her.

"So lovely," he murmured as he plucked gently at the lacy fabric, easing it farther down. When she stood before him, bare to the waist, he stepped back and gazed at her unabashedly. "You stand proudly," he said, "the way a woman should."

She smiled and, holding his gaze, drew the camisole back up and over her head. When she had discarded it on the floor at her feet, she hooked her thumbs beneath the waistband of her half-slip and slowly eased it off.

Jo had a secret indulgence which she had nurtured since the first moment she had been able to afford small luxuries. Her private passion was for exquisitely feminine lingerie. She had pampered herself with silk bikini panties and garter belts long before it had become fashionable to do so. The pleasure had been purely her own, until now.

She was rewarded by the sharp intake of David's breath. He took a step toward her, but she fended him off with a hand as she propped one foot, still in its high-heeled shoe, on the edge of a chair.

Slowly, as though she had all the time in the world, she unfastened the garters from one stocking and rolled it down, slipping it and the shoe off. She did the same to the other leg before she turned back to face him.

His eyes were locked on her with intensity, his face hardened by the rigid self-control he was exercising. She might have been frightened by the fierce struggle she sensed going on inside him if she hadn't come to trust him so completely. A hard, determined man he might be, but he also lived by an exacting standard of honor that she could well understand and appreciate.

A purely feminine confidence curved her mouth as she reached behind to unsnap the garter belt, then let it, too, fall to the floor. Left in only the tiny panties that shielded her womanhood, she met his gaze with unfeigned challenge.

David crossed the distance between them in a single stride. His big hands closed on her waist as he lifted her hard against him. With a low groan, he buried his face in the tender hollow of her throat. "You're going to drive me crazy," he murmured. "I know it already."

She let her head fall back as she laughed, giddy with her own exhilaration. Jo wasn't completely inexperienced, although very nearly so. She had tried sex as something she simply thought she ought to do, only to be very disappointed. The man involved, a classmate in graduate school, had strongly insinuated that the fault lay with her—that she was cold, unresponsive, passionless. Intellectually she had known he was wrong. Now it was very nice to discover that emotionally as well.

She wrapped her arms around him, her feet dangling above the floor, happiness bubbling through her. He was so strong in the smoothly muscled power of his body, yet there was nothing threatening in that strength. When he carried her over to the bed and put her gently down, she felt cherished and protected.

She lay on her back, her arms folded beneath her head, watching as he pulled off his shirt and hastily unfastened his belt. As he began slipping his slacks off, he laughed with a hint of self-consciousness. "You made this look easy."

"Don't tell me you've never undressed for a woman before?"

"Not exactly, but it isn't an everyday experience." He lowered himself onto the bed beside her, then stretched out with his head propped on one hand and regarded her gravely. "I think there's something you ought to know."

"What's that?" she asked.

"I'm a virgin."

Even from the inside, Jo had the definite impression that her eyes took on the aspect of twin saucers as her mouth dropped open. It took her a moment to realize that he was kidding. "Okay," he said, relenting, "maybe not exactly. But I haven't been Casanova, either. No one-night stands, and I've only had a handful of relationships. The last of them ended almost a year ago when she decided she wasn't ready for a more permanent commitment. Since then I've certainly had the urge, but not strongly enough to do anything about it. At least not until I met you."

"I'm flattered," Jo said quietly. She wasn't particularly surprised by what he was telling her—he had struck her from the beginning as a man who had too much intelligence and self-respect to feel compelled to put notches on his bedpost, or to become a notch on anyone else's. But she was struck by the fact that he was willing to speak so honestly.

And she felt compelled to do the same. "There was a man," she said softly, "several years ago. It didn't amount to much." A wry smile lit her eyes. "The fact is, it was pretty well a letdown."

"And since then?"

She shook her head. "No one. It's not that I haven't thought about it. Of course, I have. But I guess I was reluctant because of the other experience. My work provided a very convenient excuse for postponing any other entanglement."

"I understand," David said gently as he traced the line of her cheek with a solitary finger. When he pressed it over her lips, they parted slightly.

"What I'm trying to say..." she murmured.

"Is that you're afraid you don't know all the moves."

She flushed slightly, but didn't look away from him. "That's it."

"Neither do I. Besides, it doesn't matter." He leaned across her and snapped off the light, leaving the room in gentle shadows. She felt his breath warm and caressing against her as he murmured, "We'll learn them together."

Softly, without haste, he matched his actions to his words. Jo gasped beneath the intuitive touch of his hands and mouth. He seemed to know instinctively where she was most sensitive and how best to please her.

To her surprise, she seemed to know the same about him. Once she had gathered her courage and begun to caress him, tremulously at first, she found only delight in his quick response. A heady sense of confidence enveloped her as she realized that she could move him as much as he did her.

Their lovemaking changed, became far less tentative. A playful element entered in as they set out to discover all there was to know about each other.

"What happens," Jo murmured, "if I do this?"

"Nothing," David replied through gritted teeth.

"Nothing at all?" she asked as she touched him again.

"I'm immune. Ahh."

She sat back on her heels and surveyed him with a smile. "A regular man of steel."

"Part of me, anyway." He sat up partway and reached for her. "Now you're going to get yours, woman."

"Promises, promises."

"If you had any sense," he informed her as he gently levered her body beneath his, "you'd be squealing for mercy."

"Squealing? I never, positively never, squeal. Aii."

"What was that?"

"A squeal, I think." She lay back, panting slightly as the waves of pleasure he had provoked continued to reverberate through her. "My God, you should have to carry a warning label."

He tried to shrug that off, but couldn't help looking pleased. There was such joy in watching her body come alive. He could hardly believe that her experience had been as limited and as dissatisfying as she had said.

Indeed he might not have believed it except that he knew absolutely that she wouldn't lie to him. That fact itched uncomfortably at his conscience. He pushed the thought aside and turned his attention to vastly more pleasant matters.

Her breasts were small, perfectly formed and exquisitely sensitive. He had only to rake his thumbs over them to make her moan. When he suckled lightly at each of her nipples in turn, she arched her back and cried out softly.

Her response fueled his own. He knew that he couldn't possibly hold on much longer, but he was determined to do so until he was sure the experience would be perfect for her. Fueling his determination was the overwhelming need to banish the past completely from her mind, to make her forget everything except him and what they could have together.

He was already closer to achieving that than he knew. Jo writhed beneath him, her head tossing back and forth across the pillows. Her lids were tightly closed, but behind them she saw David—beautiful, passionate, tantalizing David. His name broke from her at the same moment she reached for him.

He came into her slowly and with great care, mindful of how long it had been for her and concerned that he might, however inadvertently, cause some hurt. If he did, Jo was insensible to it. She could feel nothing except the power and beauty of their joining. Nothing else mattered; nothing else existed. They were completely alone in a world of their own making.

Afterward they lay exhausted in a tangle of arms and legs, laughing softly and unable to resist dropping little kisses on whatever part of each other's bodies happened to be convenient.

"Incredible," David murmured with what he was sure was the last of his breath. Never in his most fervent imaginings would he have believed it possible to reach such heights and survive to savor the experience. Yet, savor it he did, even as he looked forward to a prompt repetition.

"Fantastic," Jo whispered against his heated skin. "I had no idea." Drowsily she added, "Think if we could bottle this."

"Our fortune would be made."

"No more war, no more nastiness. Everybody in the world would walk around in a state of languid stupor, smiling at each other."

"Sounds like a nice place," David said, gathering her to him. He reached down to pull the blanket over them both. It was still raining, and the air was cool, but in the bed there was only warmth and utter contentment.

"Our place," Jo whispered. Her eyelids felt weighted down. She tried to raise them, only to find that she could not. With a low, regretful sigh, she nestled her head in the curve of his shoulder and went to sleep.

When she awoke she was alone in the room, and the phone was ringing. She fumbled for the receiver, managing to get it to her ear enough to hear the automatic wake-up call. With a low groan, she put the phone back down and tried to gather her thoughts enough to face a new day.

The room was filled with a light that made her wince until she realized that it meant the rain was over. Having not seen the sun in several days, she should have welcomed the sight. But instead all she really wanted to do was crawl back under the covers and pull them up over her head.

Had she really been so utterly abandoned in David's arms? Had that passionate, demanding woman really been herself? She felt as though she had stepped completely out of her own character, inhabiting a different skin where she felt unaccountably at home.

Far from feeling ashamed by anything that had happened between them, she could not deny a sense of overwhelming satisfaction. She was delighted with him, with herself, with the world in general.

Until she stepped into the hall, after showering and dressing in a mindless glow, only to confront Harry Morton on a rampage. "Where the hell have you been?" the campaign manager demanded. "I've been looking all over for you."

She made a slightly bewildered gesture toward the door she had just closed. "I was in my room. Where did you think I was?"

"I thought you'd be up before now," Harry said. He was calming down slightly, though he continued to look extremely harried. "I checked the restaurant, the hair salon, one place after another." A bit sheepishly, he added, "I guess I should have just called your room."

"Why?" Jo asked as she took his arm and began surreptitiously steering him toward the elevator. "What's up?"

"Wilson, that's what. I knew that guy was going to be trouble. Didn't I tell you that right from the beginning? Didn't I say he was the Attila the Hun of the airwaves, no offense meant to Attila? Didn't I?"

"Yes," Jo said patiently even as her stomach was plummeting, "you did, Harry. Now suppose you tell me what's happened."

"I don't know. I only wish I did."

"Then why—?"

"All I know for sure is that he's in with Greeley and whatever they're talking about has the senator extremely upset. Stress on 'extremely.' I actually heard him shouting."

"Him who?"

"Greeley, of course. You think I'd care if Wilson was shouting? I don't give a damn what that guy does except when he gets in the way of my candidate. Lemme tell you, if he thinks we've come this far just so he can waltz in and screw everything up, he's got another think coming."

"I've never heard the senator even raise his voice," Jo said, "let alone shout."

"Well, he's doing it now. I couldn't make out the words exactly, but it doesn't take a genius to figure this is nothing good."

No, Jo thought, it didn't. Her throat clenched painfully as she fought to control herself. Absently she patted Harry on the arm. "I'll go see if I can find out what's happening."

"Thanks, kid," he said, giving her a look that was genuinely grateful. "Maybe I'm getting old, but I just can't take too many surprises like this. Whatever Wilson's stumbled on, I got a feeling I'd rather not know."

"It can't be anything terrible," she said quietly. "Greeley is a decent, honorable man. I'll never believe there's anything in his life that he needs to be ashamed of."

"Maybe not," Harry muttered, "but somehow Wilson's hit a nerve."

As she took the elevator up two floors to where the senator's suite was located, Jo tried to tell herself that Harry could be completely wrong. He might have mistaken a harmless, if exuberant discussion for something far more sinister.

Except that she could think of no reason for David to be meeting with the senator at such an early hour unless the matter was urgent. She remembered how preoccupied and concerned he had been the night before, and her mouth tightened.

The Secret Service agent on duty at the door of the suite stood aside to let her enter. She glanced at him, half hoping for some indication of what she would encounter, but his face was rigorously, professionally blank.

Gathering her courage, she walked into the living room. At first neither man noticed her arrival. Jason was standing in front of the windows, his back to the room. He looked tired to Jo. His shoulders were slightly stooped, something very unusual for him, and the glimpse she had of his face in profile looked almost unutterably weary.

David was sitting on the couch. He was in his usual, relaxed position, slightly slouched with his long legs stretched out in front of him. But there was an air of tension about him Jo could not ignore. She cleared her throat.

David's head jerked, and he looked at her directly. "Hello, Jo."

She forced herself to nod. "David."

The senator had turned around. He managed a wan smile. "Let me guess," he said, "Harry got you."

She shrugged as though to make light of it. "He said you were going ten rounds in here, but I figured he was exaggerating."

The two men exchanged a glance. Quietly David said, "Not really. It has been a bit heated."

There was silence for a moment, then the senator said, "Sit down, Jo. You may as well hear this."

"I don't think—" David began.

"I said for her to sit down," Greeley snapped. "For God's sake, you're planning to drag this out in front of millions of people, aren't you? What difference does it make if she hears it now?"

David started to say something, thought better of it and subsided into watchful silence. Wishing she could be anywhere else, Jo sat down.

"Look," she said as calmly as she could manage, "if something's come up, something David is concerned about, I'm sure we can work it out. It's only a matter of a simple explanation. Surely we have nothing to hide."

She said this last part directly to Greeley, looking, almost pleading for his confirmation. This was the man she had believed in implicitly for her entire professional life. The man she was working to help put into the most powerful office in the world. It was inconceivable to her that he could do or say anything that would betray her trust or the trust of millions of others like her who were already planning to vote for him.

Yet there was no denying the implacable set of David's features, the absolute will and determination she felt coming from him. He was unrelenting in his pursuit of the truth. Whatever he had confronted Greeley with demanded to be answered.

Very quietly, so that she had to strain to hear him, the senator said, "I wish I could share your confidence, Jo. Unfortunately it isn't that simple."

"Why not?" she asked.

"Because..." He hesitated a moment, looking from her to David. Finally he said, "Because Mr. Wilson wants to know why I've been blackmailed for the past ten years."

# Chapter 11

B-blackmailed?'' Jo stammered. She wished she could say something else, but nothing came out except that single, horrifying word.

Jason sighed deeply. He sat down in a chair opposite the couch and ran a hand through his thinning hair. For the first time since Jo had known him, he suddenly looked all of his forty-five years and then some.

Wearily he said, "Suppose you tell her, David."

She shifted her gaze to him. In a voice she was proud carried no emotion, she said, "Yes, suppose you do."

David shifted on the couch, gathering his thoughts. At length he said, "I've informed the senator that since I broadcast that piece a week ago indicating I was doing a story on his campaign, I've been contacted twice by a woman who claims to have received substantial payments from him over the past ten years. Blackmail is the senator's term, not mine. I simply asked him if he had an explanation.''

"And I blew up,'' Jason said ruefully.

"I don't understand,'' Jo said, looking from one man to the other. To David, she said, "You must get dozens, if not hundreds of crank tips like that. Why pay attention to that one?''

"Several reasons. To start with, the woman was absolutely rock solid on her story. When I tried to shake her on it, she held firm. There's nothing desperate or frantic about her, as is usually the case in situations like this. On the contrary, the only word I can think of to describe her is complacent. She seems to be absolutely confident she's going to get what she wants.''

"Which is?'' Jo asked.

"Publicity for herself and an end to the senator's presidential hopes.''

Jo made no attempt to hide her skepticism or her growing anger. "And you say she isn't a crank, strictly on that basis?'' she demanded.

"No,'' he told her quietly. "I've seen photostats of bank orders made out in her name. When traced, they lead straight back to the senator. They extend back over a period of ten years and were made on a regular monthly basis.''

Jo's breath caught in her throat. "There has to be a simple explanation,'' she insisted, even as her mind struggled to find one. "Even if the signature looks genuine, she could have gotten it from another source, perhaps a routine thank-you letter in return for a donation. It could have been pasted onto spurious checks and photostated in an attempt to hide what she'd done."

"Exactly what I thought," David said, "until I got in touch with the bank where the deposits were made. The original bank orders did exist, and the payments were made. Moreover the records indicate that they came from the senator's bank account."

"That's privileged information," Jo pointed out. "I'd like to know how you got it."

"I told you," he said steadily. "Through a contact, whose identity you must realize I'm not going to reveal."

"It doesn't matter," Jason interjected quietly. "Like it or not, Jo, I have to accept the fact that David has substantiated the information he was given. I did make the payments, and he knows it."

"What I don't know," David said, "is why."

"Do you care?" Jo demanded, unable to hide her bitterness. In her agitation she stood up and faced him angrily. "Does it make any difference? You've got a great story, David, exactly what you've been waiting for. Leading Presidential Candidate Admits to Being Blackmailed. You'll get great ratings, the network will love you, and you'll be able to congratulate yourself for proving once again that no one is perfect. You can wallow in your cynicism to your heart's content, if you've got one, that is."

Her voice broke. She turned away, determined not to let him see the sudden sheen of tears that blurred her vision.

She wasn't quick enough. David did see and with a muttered groan, he jumped up and strode to her side. Ignoring the senator, he put his hands on her arms and turned her to him. "I know you're upset. So am I. But you have to realize that I have a job to do."

"And that comes before anything else, doesn't it? Any human feeling, any shred of compassion, even simple decency." No longer able to prevent the tears that trickled slowly down her pale cheeks, she said, "You've known about this for days. Certainly you knew about it last night. Why in the name of God did you—"

Suddenly mindful that the senator was still in the room with them, she broke off and jerked away from David. She wrapped her arms around herself and stood stiffly, fighting against the waves of pain and disillusionment that were sweeping over her.

Through that anguish, she heard Jason Greeley speaking softly and calmly. "I have a suggestion, which I hope both of you will take very seriously. If you would care to hear it?"

Reluctantly she nodded. Beside her, David did the same.

To him, the senator said, "You haven't actually met with this woman yet, have you? You've only spoken with her on the phone?" When David nodded, he continued. "Then I think you should go meet with her."

"I'm planning to do that," David said. "But before then, I wanted to give you a chance to explain the situation yourself. That's why I came here this morning."

"I appreciate that. The problem is that I don't have the right to explain it to you. It involves certain confidences which are not mine to break." At the expression that flitted across David's face, he added, "I know that must sound like a convenient excuse to you but, believe me, it's not. If I were the only person involved, this whole situation would never have developed in the first place. But I'm not, and I'm not about to run roughshod over the feelings of another person who is very vulnerable in this regard.''

"You must realize what's at stake here," David said.

Jason nodded. "Of course I do. That's why I'm suggesting that you go speak to this woman. While you're doing that, I'm going to see if the other person involved will agree to speak with you. That's the only way you're going to get all the facts, which I'm convinced is what you really want.''

"It is," David said sincerely. He cast a quick look at Jo. "That and nothing else.''

"Then do as I suggest. When you come back in a few days, perhaps we can work this out.''

"And if we can't?'' David asked.

Jason shrugged. "Then I'll have no choice. You'll break the story, and I'll resign from the campaign.''

"Don't say that," Jo broke in. "You can't simply throw away everything you've worked for all these years. But even more importantly, you are the right man for the job. This country needs you. Doesn't that count for anything?''

He shook his head wryly. "Thank you for the vote of confidence, Jo. It means a great deal to me, especially since, under the circumstances, it speaks volumes about your loyalty and faith. But the plain fact of the matter is that no one is indispensable. The country will muddle through. It always does.''

"It deserves better than that," she murmured. The fervency of her conviction neither surprised nor embarrassed her. She was tired of the common wisdom that said everything and everyone was pretty much the same, that all gradations of political thinking were more or less equally valid, that in the final analysis things happened over which no one had any control so why worry anyway?

What that all boiled down to for her was the idea that individuals could not make any difference. She believed exactly the opposite. Moreover she believed that the difference Jason Greeley could make was absolutely vital not only to the immediate present but far into the future.

"Will you do as he asks?" she demanded of David.

"Of course I will, but with the understanding that when I see this woman, if I decide there really is a story, I can't hold it up very long."

"I'm not asking you to," Jason reminded him quietly. "However, I do have another suggestion." He was silent for a moment, looking from one of them to the other. His eyes were surprisingly tender as he said, "I think Jo should go with you."

"What?" Jo exclaimed. She couldn't even begin to imagine why such a notion would have occurred to the senator. Certainly, it hadn't to her, nor did she wish to consider it for even a moment. "I don't think that would be in any way appropriate," she murmured stiffly.

"I don't need anyone keeping tabs on me, Senator," David said. "You can be assured that I'll treat you fairly without that."

"I have no doubt that you will," Jason said equably. "I'm not suggesting that Jo go along for my sake, but rather for hers, and yours."

At their startled looks, he said, "Forgive me if I'm being too personal. Unlike presidential candidates, you two are entitled to your privacy. But I have the definite sense that something very important is happening between you and that this story has thrown a wrench into it."

"That's putting it mildly," Jo murmured. She wasn't surprised by the senator's astuteness. He had always struck her as an unusually perceptive man. But he was also normally one who steered clear of anything that could smack of intrusion into the private lives of his staff. This time, however, he apparently felt compelled to speak up.

"Just hear me out," he said when David would have objected. "I've had the benefit in my life of an unusually close and loving marriage. I've never taken that for granted, not for a moment. Even if I might have been inclined to do so, I've seen the evidence all around me of how very rare and precious such a relationship is."

Smiling at them gently, he continued. "You both may be too caught up in the events and emotions of the moment to fully appreciate what's at stake for you. That's why this is no time for you to be separated. If that happens, you're liable to both brood over the situation, your positions will harden, and the distance between you will become insurmountable. That would be a shame."

"On the other hand," David said quietly. "If Jo does come with me, we're liable to fight constantly and by the time we get back, we may not even be speaking to each other."

"In which case," Jason said, "you'll know that you really weren't suited to each other to start with. Because if you can't be tolerant and supportive of each other now, you certainly won't be able to do so later."

What he said made sense. Jo only wished that it didn't. She glanced at David, wondering how he was reacting. His expression was unreadable, but when he spoke his voice was calm and accepting. "I think you're right. If Jo will agree, I'd like her to come with me."

Put that way, she could hardly refuse. With a quick nod she signified her acceptance.

"The woman's name is Martha James," David said. "She lives in Nevada, outside of Las Vegas. There was a report on the news this morning that the mechanics are about to settle, so we ought to be able to get a flight out of Boston sometime today."

"I only need a few minutes to pack," Jo murmured. When she had found herself on the road unexpectedly, she had picked up a few necessities, but they all fit neatly into one small bag. She knew that David traveled equally lightly and tried not to read anything into that. It would have been unfair to conclude that he preferred to go through life emotionally unencumbered, but the temptation to do so was there, and she had a hard time resisting it.

As they left the senator's suite and walked down the hallway, he said quietly, "Before we go anywhere, Jo, I really think we should talk."

She hesitated, knowing that it was the right thing to do but afraid nonetheless. He was better with words than she was. They were the tools of his trade, and he used them with relentless skill. She wasn't exactly a slouch herself, and when necessary she could be extremely persuasive. But that was when her emotions were not so overwhelmingly engaged.

Back home, amid a family that loved her for all that she was different from them, understanding and acceptance had flowed at an almost subconscious level. There had been little need for words when a smile, a hug, a nod communicated far more easily and accurately.

With David, such harmony did not yet exist and might never. They needed to speak openly if they were to have any chance at all. She acknowledged that, even as she realized that she simply wasn't ready to do so. The shock of what had happened both the night before and that morning was still too great for her to be able to effectively muster her thoughts and confront him directly. She needed time first to adjust to the situation.

When she told him that, he listened quietly, then nodded. "All right. I can't say that I like it, but I understand. Only please, don't jump to any conclusions about us until we've at least had a chance to work this out."

She promised him that she wouldn't. The pledge was made in good faith even as she realized the difficulty of keeping it. Like it or not, she was hurt and frightened by what was happening between them. It seemed as though they had no sooner come together, than they had hurtled off in opposite directions at remorseless speed.

"I'm really not sure this is a good idea," she said a short time later as they were getting into the rental car to head for Boston and the airport. "I realize that the senator means well, but he's asking a lot, throwing us together like this."

"He's a very perceptive man," David said. He tossed his bag in the back seat along with hers and got in behind the wheel.

"You sound surprised." She couldn't resist a slight smile. The idea of David being forced to reassess his opinions about politicians in general, and the senator in particular, didn't disturb her at all.

"I suppose I am," he admitted as he started the car and they pulled away from the curb. "He understands more about people than I'd expected."

"Did you believe what he said about his marriage?"

David nodded. "Yes, I did. I don't know his wife personally, but the general impression seems to be that they really are devoted to each other. That's sufficiently unusual to be commented upon."

She leaned her head back against the seat and closed her eyes. The tension of the morning's revelations was taking its toll. She was tired, and part of her wanted nothing so much as to slip away into the protection of unconsciousness.

"Go to sleep if you want," David said quietly. "I'll wake you up when we get there."

She shook her head. "If I sleep now, I'll be out of kilter all day."

He smiled faintly. "Are you sure it isn't that you just don't trust my driving?"

"You seem to know what you're doing."

He glanced at her and nodded. "Yes, I do."

She was silent for several moments before she said, "I don't really think you should have turned away from this story, David, if in fact there is a story. I know I suggested that in the senator's suite, but it was out of line."

Her admission surprised him. He hadn't expected it and didn't quite know how to respond. Finally he said, "I understand why you felt the way you did. It must have come as a tremendous shock to you."

"At first, but I'm convinced there's an explanation that will in no way discredit Jason. He as good as told you that when he said it wasn't his confidence to break."

"He's protecting someone else," David agreed. "Do you have any idea who?"

"I'm sure we're both of the same opinion about that. The obvious choice is Marianne. It's not just a coincidence that he picked that moment to remind you of how much he loves her."

David shook his head slowly. "I've got to admit that I can't imagine what she could possibly have been involved in that would justify what he's done."

"That's what Martha James is supposed to tell us," she reminded him quietly. For good measure, she added, "Provided that what she says is true."

Several moments passed before David said, "You find this whole thing very distasteful, don't you?"

She turned to him, her gaze steady and intent. "Of course I do. How could anyone possibly find it otherwise? You said yourself that she's acting from the most selfish motives. She wants to hurt, and she wants attention. Without you, or someone like you, she couldn't achieve either."

"We're both jumping to conclusions about Martha James," he said quietly, not taking offense at what she had said about his role.

It was true that the mere existence of the media tended to be a catalyst for certain people to do things they might otherwise not have done. That was why basic rules had been developed in the past few years regarding the coverage given to terrorists. Some groups had been known to stage incidents solely to get publicity.

A very fine line had to be walked between the need to discourage such behavior and the right of the public to know when it was occurring. David didn't claim to be comfortable with that, but he accepted it and did his best to behave responsibly.

"I don't have your objectivity," Jo said quietly. "To put it very simply, that isn't my job. I'm going along on this because I think Jason is right. For us to be separated right now would put an end to any chance we may have. But that doesn't mean I can view Martha James as anything more than a corrupt, contemptible person."

"If I don't hear what she has to say," he reminded her, "then somebody else will."

"I know," Jo murmured. She fell silent, looking out the window and thinking about the terrible harm the unknown woman could do, not only to the presidential hopes of a truly deserving man, but also to herself and David.

After the night they had spent together, she was ready to admit, if only inwardly, that she loved him.

But if he destroyed the ideals that were the basis for
her life, she doubted that she would ever be able to
forgive him.

# Chapter 12

After the days of rain in Washington and along the east coast, the unrelenting sunlight of Las Vegas was all but blinding. Jo shielded her eyes as they stepped from the airport terminal into a wave of incandescent heat that caused the air to shimmer. Clusters of tourists milled around, those coming pushing their way past those who were going.

Glancing at them, Jo thought it wasn't difficult to tell the difference. The new arrivals were buoyant, laughing, self-conscious, eager to get started on the fulfillment of their expectations, whatever they might be. Those who were leaving were more subdued and appeared tired, somewhat let down, as though they were remembering once again the ordinariness of their lives.

Not everyone who came to Las Vegas gambled. She knew that, but she also knew that those who refrained were few and far between. It was, after all, the principal reason for the existence of the city that had risen out of the desert. It was a place cut off from the rest of reality, whose citizens valued it for its transient quality.

"Have you been here before?" she asked David as they got into the cab that would take them to their hotel. She had waited for him while he went to a pay phone to call Martha James. There had been no answer at the number she had given him, so they would have to try again.

He nodded as he glanced out the window at the flat, colorless land split by the black line of tarmac down which they were speeding. "Once, a couple of years ago."

"What did you think of it?"

He shrugged. "It serves a purpose."

"Which is?"

"An escape, a retreat, a chance to grab hold of fortune's wheel and try to make it spin in your favor. People need that."

"I suppose...."

The doubt he heard in her voice surprised him. He realized that there was something about this place that troubled her, whereas he had never considered it to have any particular significance, good or bad. Like so much else, it simply was. His critical faculties, acute as they were, were reserved for those things he thought actually mattered. Everything that could be said or written about the frantic, banal, vaguely sad existence of Las Vegas had already been aired. He had nothing to add to it, and he therefore dismissed it from his mind.

But now he realized that Jo was troubled. That mattered even if the cause itself did not.

"What bothers you about this place?" he asked as he placed a hand over hers. In the cab's air-conditioning, her skin was cool beneath his own. He thought of how she had felt beneath him in the heat of love and had to forcibly drag his mind away from the images that provoked.

"It seems so futile," she said at last, with a small smile of apology for saying anything so obvious.

"To you, but not to everyone. Plenty of people come here simply for fun. I'm not saying they don't care whether they win or lose, but they have a good time either way."

She shook her head, as though the gesture might shift her jumbled thoughts into some semblance of order. "It isn't only the gambling. I'm not actually against that, although I think people should be careful not to get sucked in so deeply that they can't stop when they should."

She looked out the window again. They were passing a low stretch of buildings on the outskirts of the city. She noticed a motel, a couple of diners and two places that advertised themselves as chapels offering weddings around the clock.

"It's the trivializing of everything in a place like this that bothers me. People can be married in a matter of minutes, money can be lost—or won—just as quickly, everything moves at breakneck speed and nothing counts for anything. Except that the consequences are real enough. People can end up living with them for a long time to come."

He curled his fingers around hers, increasing the pressure of his touch slightly. "You're thinking about Greeley and the consequences of what he's done."

Softly, so that her lips moved almost without sound, she said, "I'm thinking about us, too. What we shared was important to me, David. Probably more important than you know. I don't want to see it become something small and regrettable."

He was silent for several moments, letting her words sink into him. She had needed courage to speak so honestly, to let him know that he mattered so much to her at a time when she might reasonably be expected to be pulling back from him. That reassured him even as he knew that nothing was settled between them, and that he might still regret it when it finally was.

"I wish—" he began, only to break off, staring at her. The sunlight filtering through her short curls made the rich, dark brown hair look alive with a golden radiance. Her gray eyes had the sheen of silver. She naturally possessed a complexion of the sort that was usually produced by cosmetics. Her cheeks were slightly flushed and her lips, when his gaze settled at last on them, were parted.

He cleared his throat, but when he spoke, his voice was still husky. "I wish we had met at another time, another place, when things would have been different."

"We would still have been the same people," she reminded him gently, "with the same convictions and the same concerns."

Their eyes met. He saw understanding in hers that he had not expected and was encouraged by it. "Jo...I want things to work out between us. It isn't true, what you said about my not realizing how important what's happened is to you. I do realize because it's every bit as important to me. You're important. Please try to keep that in mind in the next few days.''

"I will," she promised him, looking away quickly so that he would not see how moved she was, and how afraid.

Their hotel was in the center of the Las Vegas strip, at the heart of the glittering, extravagant city within a city, which was all the tourists usually saw or cared about. But in daylight the neon was dimmed, the heat haze alternately blurred and emphasized the contours of the buildings that squatted sullenly beneath the unrelenting sun, and the street looked virtually deserted.

Inside the hotel it was different. People clustered about in the ornate lobby, meeting friends, trying to decide what to do next or simply making their way from their rooms to the casino. Jo knew that some would never leave the hotel from the day they arrived to the day they left. If they did so at all, it would be to wander down the strip to the next hotel, the next casino, the next set of roulette wheels and slot machines.

Jo wasn't interested in any such excursions. Once in her room, which was next door to David's, she unpacked and made a quick inventory of what she needed to augment her scanty baggage. She had no idea when she would be able to get back to Washington. Whatever was going to happen to the senator and the campaign, she would have to be on hand.

David had mentioned that he had phone calls to make—to the network in New York and to Martha

James, again. She left him to it as she went back
downstairs to the arcade of shops she had noticed
when they arrived. Within a short time, she was able
to purchase several pairs of slacks, a wraparound
skirt, two T-shirts and a blouse. On an optimistic note,
she tossed in a bathing suit and cover-up. It might be
that she wouldn't have time to use them, but she hoped
otherwise.

After she had returned to her room, she put through
a call to Shelley who, in her own and the senator's absence, was holding down the fort.

"This place is like a tomb," the older woman said
with a laugh. "Congress may be officially in session,
but there is absolutely nothing going on. All anyone
wants to think about are the conventions. Still it
wouldn't be a bad idea if the senator could swing back
this way next week. The vote's coming up on that defense bill, and he needs to be on hand for it."

"Have you mentioned that to him?" Jo asked. She
knew that Shelley and the senator spoke on an aver-
age of once a day and was curious to know if she had
talked with him since David dropped the Martha
James bombshell. She wanted to know the senator's
mood, but could hardly ask about it directly.

"He says he's not sure of his schedule at this point,"
Shelley said with a note of exasperation. "I know he's
due to be back here so what's the problem?"

Jo hesitated. She disliked the idea of keeping anything so important from her colleague. That worry
was heightened by the fact that Shelley might well be
resenting her own isolation in Washington while Jo
traveled with the campaign. Still she believed that the

fewer people who had such sensitive information, the better.

Shelley would never deliberately leak a confidence, but she was in more or less constant touch with the reporters covering the Senate, and any sudden change in her demeanor would be noted by them. In this most political of seasons when nothing seemed to matter except the coming election, every candidate's staff was under close scrutiny. Let a single aide show a spurt of anxiety, and the rumor mill would start churning away.

Accordingly she decided to err on the side of tact. "No problem, but you know as well as I do that the schedule is always approximate. Maybe he's just feeling a little tired and is thinking of taking a few days at home for a change."

"Could be," Shelley agreed. "Well, listen, if anything changes, let me know. But in the meantime, enjoy the tour. At least you're back to flying now."

Jo promised to keep in touch, chatted a few more minutes and then hung up. Only after she had set the receiver down did she realize that she had deliberately given Shelley no idea where she was. Her absence from the campaign was bound to be noticed. The staffers on the road might presume she had simply returned to Washington, while the people there might think she was on the road. But sooner or later the two groups were going to realize that she was in neither place. Before that happened, she had to hope the situation would be resolved.

There was another call she wanted to make, but she hesitated before doing so. She hadn't spoken to Francis since calling from New York to tell him that she would be staying with the campaign for a while. He had assured her then that both he and Wilson were doing well and that he would look after her apartment. Strictly speaking it wasn't necessary for her to be in contact again, but she remembered how ill he had been the previous winter and felt a jolt of concern. Rather than dwell on it, she picked up the receiver.

Francis answered on the third ring. He sounded strong, and there was a note of amusement in his voice. "My dear," he said, "how are you? I understand the weather's been miserable in New England. Are you holding up all right?"

"Fine," she assured him, feeling the same twinge of guilt that she had with Shelley about not being straightforward as to her whereabouts. "How's everything there?"

"Well, let's see now. That little beast you left with me has decided he doesn't care for tuna after all. He prefers poached salmon, breast of chicken and beef filet. A very discerning fellow, all in all."

"I should have known," Jo said with a laugh. "Did you give any thought at all to feeding him plain cat food?"

"Of course not. I don't eat plain people food, so I don't see why he should do worse. Besides, he's excellent company. You know, I was going to wait to mention this to you until you got home, but if you haven't absolutely got your heart set on keeping him, I wouldn't mind doing so."

"That's a wonderful idea," Jo said. "It isn't that I don't like him; fact is, he caught on with me pretty quickly. But I'm gone all day and I really think it would be better for him to have company. Besides, haven't you always liked cats?''

"Always," Francis confirmed. "But my late wife was allergic to them so it's been many years since I actually kept one." He paused for a moment, then gave a rich chuckle. "I suppose now I really am a crusty old man, complete with a cat to warm my hearth."

"Oh, I don't know about that," Jo told him. "I've got the impression there's plenty of life in you yet." At least she wanted there to be. Men like Francis should, in her opinion, live out their final years exuberantly, sharing the wisdom they had accumulated over a lifetime and not, as Dylan Thomas said, "go gentle into that good night."

While there was certainly nothing wrong with her landlord taking Wilson in and giving him a good home, the little kitten was hardly a sufficient outlet for Francis's warm, giving nature. He had children whom he cared for deeply, but none lived near Washington, and he saw them only seldom over the course of a year. As was so often the case with people who lived into their seventies, many of his closest friends had passed away.

Though he was still greatly respected in the capital, it was a distant sort of honor. He no longer had, nor in all likelihood would want, a role in actual decision making. But he must not be allowed to become isolated, as older people who had lost their spouses and lived far from their children too often tended to be.

Jo privately resolved to do something about that when she got back to Washington. Of course, she wouldn't breathe a word of her intentions to Francis. He would be offended by anything that smacked of pity, however erroneous any suspicion of that would be. She did not pity him in the least, but she did sympathize with the changes recent years had brought to his life, and as a friend she wanted to help ease them.

Exactly how she could go about that, she didn't know, but it kept her mind usefully occupied for some time after she got off the phone. While she took a shower and put on a pair of her new slacks and a T-shirt, she was conscious of biding her time, trying to keep the tension at bay as she waited for David.

A glance at her watch confirmed that he had had ample opportunity to do everything he had said he was going to do. She had indeed expected him to rejoin her before then and was hoping he had been able to contact Martha James. The sooner they could speak with the woman, the sooner they could leave. Nothing would please her better.

But when she knocked on the door joining their two rooms, there was no answer. Nor could she hear him on the phone talking when she, with some hesitation, put her ear to the door.

She was just beginning, however reluctantly, to consider the possibility that he might have gone on without her when there was a knock at her door. She hurried to answer it and found David standing in the hall. In his hand was a bouquet of flowers.

"What's this?" she asked, as she stood aside to let him in.

"I was downstairs looking for a newspaper when I noticed that they have a florist here. Nice, don't you think?"

"Lovely," Jo said as she took the bouquet. In among the irises and tulips were tiny pink roses that gave off a delightful fragrance. She breathed it in deeply while she tried to come to terms with the rather touching gesture David had just made.

She couldn't remember the last time anyone had given her flowers. If a woman was married, she might get them on her birthday or anniversary. If she had children, there was always Mother's Day. But a single woman, especially one living in a city like Washington where the men tended to be just the teeniest bit arrogant, rarely saw a flower unless she bought it for herself.

Yet David had brought her the bouquet. "Thank you," she said softly as she looked around for something to put it in. She didn't feel quite ready to meet his eyes, suspecting what he would see in hers. They had already spoken of their mutual regret for the circumstances that had arisen between them. There was no reason to do so again.

There was no vase in the room, but there was a bucket meant to hold ice, which turned out to be a perfectly suitable substitute. After Jo had filled it with water and arranged the flowers, she set them in the center of the round table near the windows. They went a long way toward brightening the dull, plastic contours of the room.

With an effort, she brought her mind back to the matter at hand. "Were you able to reach Martha James?"

David shook his head. "There's still no answer. The problem is that I've got no street address; otherwise we could just go over there and take our chances. Her phone number is unlisted, and I don't have the kind of contacts with the phone company here that could help out. But I'm working on that through a friend at the network."

"Is that how you got to the bank?" Jo asked. She couldn't help herself. She was still offended by the fact that he had been able to trace the checks so easily. Not that she wasn't perfectly well aware that such things could happen. It was simply the first time she had come face-to-face with such a breach of confidentiality.

"It really bothers you, doesn't it?" David asked gently.

"That you found out something that is supposed to be kept secret except from people authorized to know? Yes, that bothers me."

"To tell you the truth, it does me, too."

She looked at him in surprise. "Then why—?"

"Did I do it? Why did I pursue the information if doing so struck me as wrong?" She nodded. "Because we don't live in an ideal world. Because sometimes we all have to do things we're not exactly happy with. Most of all because I felt an obligation to discover if there was any truth to what Martha James was claiming. If I'd turned up dry with the bank, chances are I would have written her off, and that would have been that."

"So it was expedient," she said softly. "That's it?"

He shrugged, not comfortable with the term but not apologetic, either. "There is no way that the kind of information I turned up from the bank would ever form the sole basis for any story that I might do. All it told me was that there might be a story after all. The senator confirmed that when he admitted to making the payments."

"For a very good reason," Jo reminded him.

"Which he isn't at liberty to divulge, at least not right now." They stared at each other for a moment before he smiled and held out a hand. "Look, we can go 'round and 'round about this, or we can go downstairs and get something to eat. Which will it be?"

Jo hesitated, but only for a moment. She, too, smiled as she started for the door. "I'm starved. Let's eat."

# Chapter 13

It served her right, Jo decided. She had disliked Las Vegas at first sight, judging it to be superficial, artificial and in the final analysis, decadent. Only now did she discover that it contained such a place as Cowboy Bob's.

As she looked down at the steaming plate of baby back ribs in front of her, she fought a brief but foregone battle with her conscience. So her clothes would end up a bit tighter than she liked. So what? Once she was back in Washington, she would sweat the extra weight off quickly enough. Besides, she had long since resigned herself to the fact that she was never going to be sylphlike.

"Pass the coleslaw, please," she said with a resigned grin.

David did as she asked. They were sitting at a table for two that was covered with a red-and-white check-

erboard cloth and set with utilitarian white plates.
There was a metal container of paper napkins and a
salt-and-pepper set in one corner of the table. A jukebox was mounted on the wall above. From farther
down the row of booths, good country fiddle music
was playing.

Jo finished a rib, licked her fingers and helped herself to the coleslaw. Cowboy Bob's was crowded.
Every table was taken, and there were people lined up
at the door. They'd been lucky to get seated as quickly
as they had.

Most of the diners were tourists, but here and there
were people she suspected were locals. They were
dressed less flamboyantly than the others, chinos and
cotton shorts being the rule instead of Hawaiian print
T-shirts and Bermuda shorts. They tended to concen-
trate more strictly on the food, aside from exchang-
ing a quiet word or two with the waitresses. Regardless
of age or sex, many of them had faces that were
heavily tanned and weathered.

The exceptions were the show girls. There was a table full of them not far from where Jo and David were
seated. When they had walked in all conversation had
ceased for a moment. Not until the statuesquely tall,
lushly endowed young women had taken their seats
had the normal buzz of activity picked up again.

Jo watched them surreptitiously. The girls really did
have beautiful bodies, as well as extravagant hair in a
vast range of colors, many of which weren't found in
nature. But when she zeroed in on their faces, she realized that only one or two of them could really be
called pretty. The rest looked perfectly ordinary,
though she doubted most people ever noticed.

The girls talked quietly among themselves, ignoring the tourists who continued to stare with very little discretion. Like herself. Embarrassed by her curiosity, she glanced away only to find David watching her.

"See how easy it is?" he said.

"What do you mean?"

"Something catches your attention, and the next thing you know you're focusing in on it, excluding everything else, even whatever little voice in the back of your mind might be telling you that you aren't behaving properly. Reporters don't, you know. Behave properly, I mean. That isn't what we're paid for."

"You're paid to question?"

He nodded and raised a hand for the waitress. When he caught her eye, he gestured for her to bring two more beers. "That's the job," he said. "You get up in the morning asking 'why' and you keep on doing it right through the day. Sometimes you're still asking it in your sleep. I know that's what's been happening to me lately."

"About Greeley?" Jo asked, though she was certain she already knew the answer.

David knew that she did, too, but he nodded anyway. "He could have denied what I had. When he got angry, I thought he was going to. It passed through his mind."

"You can't know that," she protested. "Nobody ever knows what goes on in somebody else's mind."

"I'm still sure it occurred to him. He was taken by surprise. His first reaction was desperation, and he was fumbling around for something to grab hold of. When he couldn't find anything, that's when he got angry."

"That's very unusual for him," she said quietly. "He's normally a very equable man, very calm but never with any suggestion of excessive control that might spell trouble. I've always thought of him as a man who simply knew himself well, both his strengths and his weaknesses."

"Which would you say his wife is?"

Jo ignored her first impulse to spring to Marianne's defense and forced herself to think objectively. "You heard what he said about his marriage."

"That's true, but a man can be devoted to a woman who isn't any good for him. It's happened often enough."

"Not in this case," Jo said firmly. "I won't claim that I know Marianne very well. She's too busy with her family and with her own interests to be well-known to anyone on the staff. But I am sure that she's a basically solid, stable person. Moreover nobody could ever convince me that she doesn't love her husband as much as he loves her."

"Then why," David asked quietly, "has she let him get into a situation that may destroy him?"

Jo was silent for a moment, wrestling with her fears that he was right. Slowly she said, "You're presuming that Marianne is at the heart of this. She may have nothing to do with it at all. There are the children, other relatives, friends. There could be any number of explanations."

"Possibly," David agreed. He looked at her directly across the table's width. "He could also be lying. There might not be anyone else involved at all. He might simply have said there was in order to stall for time."

"No," she said emphatically. "That I can't believe."

He shrugged and wiped his hands on a paper napkin. "We'll know soon enough, anyway, once I reach Martha."

But another try at getting her on the phone as they were leaving the restaurant failed. "This is getting ridiculous," David said. He dug his hands into the pockets of his slacks and stared off into space, his broad shoulders slightly hunched. "It's as though she's dodging me."

Jo felt the worry in him and was moved to tenderness by it. All right, they were on opposite sides of the fence in this matter. But he was the man she cared about, very deeply, and he was hurting. She couldn't ignore that.

As she put a hand on his arm, she said quietly, "Martha will turn up. She may not have understood that you were going to be here today."

David didn't correct her, although he knew that he had made his plans perfectly clear to the woman. He could still hear her satisfied chuckle when he announced he was coming.

"I'll try again later," he said. "In the meantime, how about a little sight-seeing?"

Jo agreed, though it was still hot. The sun had gone down several hours before, but that didn't seem to make any difference. The air still seemed to be simmering with heat, and the neon lights attached to every building effectively banished the dark.

They walked slowly up the street toward their hotel. There was relatively little to be seen along the way, only a series of hotels and casinos that seemed virtually indistinguishable to Jo. They passed spraying fountains lit by colored lights, rows of limousines parked with their engines running and their air conditioners on and lines of tourist buses whose bored drivers sat with newspapers spread out over the steering wheels.

The action continued inside. "I suppose," Jo said as they walked into the hotel lobby, "that it's silly to come all the way to Las Vegas and not go to a casino once."

"Might as well take a look," David agreed, "though I've got to tell you, I don't think you'll be impressed."

He was right. Jo stood for a few minutes watching the people at the slot machines mechanically insert quarters and pull down the levers until she became almost hypnotized by the repetitive action. She was sure that they were, too. While she was watching, a bell went off, and a young woman suddenly began squealing and jumping up and down. She held her hands out as quarters began spewing out onto the floor. A casino employee came over with a bucket while others discreetly shooed away any of those who might have been tempted to poach.

"A hundred dollars," the young woman exclaimed as she stared at the money. "I can't believe it. A hundred dollars!"

Several other people gathered around the machines murmured their congratulations. A minute or so later they were back pulling the levers. The young woman stood uncertainly, looking around as though she wasn't sure what she was supposed to do now that she had won. The answer occurred to her quickly enough.

Jo watched as she began to dip her hand into the
bucket at her feet, taking the quarters she had won and
shoveling them back into the machine. Not the same
one she'd won from; at least she had that much sense.

"Let's check out the tables," David said. He took
her arm and led her away. The look of distress on her
face as she watched the people betting bothered him.
He accepted that Jo was an intelligent and sensitive
woman with a great deal of compassion for others, but
her reaction seemed excessive.

"It's legal, you know," he said only half-
facetiously, thinking that it wouldn't be a bad idea to
remind her. "And there are plenty of people who enjoy gambling without ever getting hurt in the least by
it. They set a budget before they get here, stick to it
and have fun in the process. Where's the harm?"

"For them? There isn't any. I know that. It's the
others who bother me." She glanced around at the
roulette tables with their swiftly spinning wheels and
at the people pressed up against them, watching intently. Softly she said, "I had an uncle who gambled.
Not because he wanted to or because he thought it was
fun, but because he was well and truly hooked. He lost
everything in the process: his wife, his kids, everything. I have no idea if he's even still alive."

"Did he ever try to get help?"

Jo nodded. "My father was always after him, and
I think a couple of times he did try to do something
about it, but he never succeeded. Something would
happen and he'd slip right back in. He had a stake in
the ranch that my father only managed to save by
buying it from him. Dad insisted on giving the money
to Aunt Liz, and he actually got my uncle to agree to

that in one of his rare periods of reform. But it didn't last any longer than the others had. At least Aunt Liz wasn't left completely broke.''

"I can understand now why this place bugs you," he said gently. "With a problem like that in your family, you're bound to think the worst of gambling." Firmly he said, "Let's get out of here."

She looked at him in surprise. "We don't have to, if you want to stay. It's true I don't think this is great, but I don't have to run from it, either."

"We've got enough to deal with on this trip without adding to it. Let's take in a show or go for a swim or . . ." He broke off, thinking about what he would really like to be doing and wondering if she could read his mind.

Jo had a fair idea of what was passing behind those dark brown eyes. He was looking at her with what a certain sort of novel would describe as brooding intensity. It startled her a bit to realize that she didn't mind at all.

Craziness. That was what that was. Out of the frying pan into the fire. Surely she had enough sense to keep her distance from him until the problems between them were resolved one way or the other? Surely she had that much self-control?

Maybe, maybe not. Because she heard herself saying, "The shows are probably all booked. I'm for the swim instead."

She was counting on there being other people in the pool even at that late hour, but there weren't. When they came back down from their rooms in their swimsuits, they had the place to themselves.

The pool's underwater lights cast an eerie glow, and the looming shape of the hotel was obscured by shadows. What room lights were on were hidden behind thickly lined curtains that blocked out the darkness.

Jo slipped off her cover-up and left it on a lounge chair near the edge of the pool. In the elevator David had worn a knit shirt as propriety dictated even in Las Vegas where bare-breasted show girls were the norm. He pulled it off over his head, giving Jo a distracting view of his broad, muscled torso. The memory of him beneath her hands and mouth raised heat within her. To escape it, she turned and jumped into the pool.

The water wasn't really cold, but by comparison to the warm air it was a shock. She surfaced, gasping and shaking droplets from her short curls. "How's the water?" David asked.

She swallowed a smile and widened her eyes innocently. "Like a bathtub."

He nodded and made a clean dive from the side of the pool. When he came up an instant later, she read a definite threat in his eyes. "Bathtub?" he all but shouted. "Ice bath would have been more like it."

A fit of the giggles seized her at the sight of the big man bearing down on her with clear intent to attack. Her laughter impeded her attempted escape, though she did manage to put half the width of the pool between them before he caught her. Then she wiggled in his arms, laughing, as he put on his best villainous face and said, "Now I'll have my way with you, my girl. See if I don't."

"Don't count on it," she warned and slipped down the length of him, darting away underwater. David followed. They romped from one end of the pool to the other and back again, teasing each other, feinting and dodging, laughing all the while. Several times their bodies, coolly wet, came into contact. She felt his growing hardness and her own arousal. Deliberately she blanked out the small voice crying caution in her mind.

"Hey, down there," somebody hollered from above, "what's the matter? Can't get a room? You gotta flop around in the pool all night?"

"Oh, dear," Jo murmured, "we're disturbing people."

David shrugged, not particularly concerned. He was feeling too good to worry much about anything. "Guy should have his windows closed. Doesn't he know how hot it is?"

"Hot," Jo repeated to herself as she watched David brace his arms on the side of the pool and pull himself out in a smooth, easy motion. When he turned and held out a hand to help her, she took it without thinking.

Once again their bodies touched but this time far more lingeringly. They stood on the edge of the water, their arms around each other. Jo raised her head and stared straight into his eyes. "David," she whispered, "what are we doing?"

"Being crazy," he said, echoing her own earlier thoughts. Then he bent his head and kissed her long and deeply.

She didn't even try to resist. The urge to do so simply wasn't in her. The stark truth of their situation did not elude her. They might have very little time left together, and it would be pointless to waste it.

They stood apart only long enough to put on their outer clothes. They walked to the elevator hand in hand. Neither spoke; there was no need to. But when they reached Jo's door, David did hesitate for a moment. She knew that he did so to give her one last chance to change her mind, and she loved him all the more for it.

But whatever sorrow and regret might lie at the end of their road together, she couldn't seek to protect herself by withdrawing from him prematurely. That would be to deny the best and strongest parts of her soul. With a slight smile, she took his hand and led him inside.

## Chapter 14

David propped himself up on an elbow and gazed at the woman asleep by his side. Jo was curled up beneath the sheet, her knees bent and one hand lying palm up beside her head. Thick lashes fanned out over her cheeks, hiding the eyes that short hours before had been luminous with passion and fulfillment. Her skin was still slightly flushed, and her lips were a bit swollen.

He smiled bemusedly as he remembered their lovemaking. It had begun tenderly enough with an air of tentativeness and caring. But quickly, fiercer emotions had seized them both. What followed astounded him, even in recollection. Never had he imagined that he could feel so rampant a need to both possess and be possessed.

In the darkness of her bed, sheltered and apart from all the rest of the world, he had sought to know her as completely as a man could ever know a woman. Her body was a wondrous thing to him, slender, soft, compelling. He had explored her inch by inch, learning the taste and texture of her like a blind man seeking sustenance.

That she had allowed such intimacy stunned him as much as his own driving need to bring it about. In all his prior experience, such as it was, no woman had ever let down the barriers of her separate self so completely. Jo held nothing back from him; she gave herself completely. In the process, he had found himself emboldened to do the same.

There was great vulnerability in such giving. In retrospect he was surprised that some innate instinct to protect himself from harm hadn't caused him to draw back. But if any such instinct had even been present in him, it hadn't managed to make itself known. For a timeless moment, he had been completely lifted out of his own being and made one with Jo. That was at once the most intensely sensual and the most spiritual experience he had ever known.

She slept deeply. No dreams appeared to disturb her rest. He was tired himself and was surprised that he wasn't also asleep. But a heady exhilaration kept rest at bay. That and fear.

He was hardly a coward, having faced both physical and moral dilemmas in his life from which a lesser man might have shrunk. But the thought that he might still lose her terrified him. In the privacy of his own mind, he could admit that without shame.

The temptation to solve the problem quickly and expediently was strong in him. All he had to do was walk away from the story. Let some other reporter hear whatever it was that Martha James had to say. Greeley might go down the tubes anyway, but at least it wouldn't be on his head. On the contrary, he could stand by to lend support and comfort to Jo in what would certainly be a devastating time for her.

There was only one problem with that scenario. It called for him to give up what was just about his sole genuine belief, namely that there was such a thing as truth, and that it was important. People, Jo included, called him a cynic, and there was something to that. He was naturally suspicious of people who sought power. He tended to think the worst of their motives until the truth proved to be otherwise. Experience had taught him that.

Jo, on the other hand, tended to think the best until forced to change her mind. He wasn't calling her naive, exactly, but for all her work in Washington, she had seen relatively little of the less attractive side of human nature. Greeley did abide by a strict code of ethics, that much David believed. What he questioned was the genuineness of the code, how intrinsic a part of the man it was or how much it merely represented the clever machinations of a politician who sensed what would please the voters.

Maybe he was being unfair. He was the first to admit the possibility. But damn it, Greeley wasn't running for dogcatcher. Brush aside everything else a president could do, and you were still left with the fact that it was his finger on the button. Any misjudgments on his part could literally lead to a cataclysm. Such a man simply had to live up to a tougher standard than other people. That was part of the job.

He turned over on his back and lay looking up at the ceiling. His body was completely relaxed, but his mind was working on overdrive. What it came down to was that he wanted it both ways. He wanted the story and he wanted Jo. Moreover he wanted her to admire and approve of what he was doing.

A tall order. He shook his head ruefully at his own presumption. Surely if he'd learned anything at all over the years it was that life was a continual series of compromises. Nobody, absolutely nobody, ever got everything he wanted. Not, of course, that any such consideration stopped people from trying.

He certainly couldn't, especially not now. He closed his eyes and an image flickered behind them. His tenth birthday. Elizabeth Stewart had brought him a cake, chocolate with chocolate icing. Candles were flickering on it. "Make a wish, David," she had said. He remembered squeezing his eyes shut so tightly that they hurt. And he remembered what he had wished.

He opened his eyes and looked at Jo again. She was still asleep. He had a feeling he'd be joining her soon since he was finally getting drowsy. Not so much though that he couldn't appreciate the irony embedded in his memories.

The wish hadn't even been put in words, so basic was it. He'd thrown out into the darkness and the flickering flames the frantic, driving child's need to some day count for something. To no longer be helpless or unwanted or looked down on because of factors over which he'd had absolutely no control. To matter, to be worthy, to be loved.

It had all been so formless then, back when he'd had no idea of what he was really asking for. Now he knew. It was lying beside him in the shape of a beautiful, strong, gentle woman. A woman he was very afraid he was going to hurt, and who would then, inevitably hurt him, possibly more than he might be able to bear.

When David woke up it was early morning. He was still lying on his back and he felt stiff, as though he hadn't turned over often enough in the night. He sat up slowly, emerging from dreams he knew he didn't want to remember.

The shower was running. As he listened, it was turned off and after a moment, Jo emerged from the bathroom. She was wrapped in a skimpy towel that didn't come much more than an inch or so down her thighs. She held the towel with one hand while with the other she vigorously dried her curls.

Seeing that he was sitting up in the bed, she gave him a smile that was only a little wary. "You're awake."

He nodded. "Finally. What time is it?"

She glanced at the clock on the table, near the flowers. "Almost seven."

"I should call New York, see if they've come up with somebody at the phone company here." He was speaking automatically; that was the last thing he wanted to do.

Jo gave up drying her hair and let her arm drop to her side. Her bare shoulders rose and fell. "Even if they have, you won't be able to reach anybody here for another couple of hours."

"True," he said, holding her eyes. She looked so sleek and sexy, standing there wrapped in the small excuse for a towel and nothing else. He, on the other hand, felt rumpled, still dazed by sleep and unmistakably aroused.

"How about breakfast?" she asked, staying where she was.

"Fine." He pulled back the sheet and got out of bed. Her eyes widened when she saw his state, and he laughed as he walked toward her. Laughed because he saw that her surprise came from pleasure and anticipation. "How hungry are you?" he asked as he came to stand before her.

Her gaze raked over him unabashedly, lingering on the broad, muscled expanse of his chest, the narrowness of his waist and the flatness of his abdomen before drifting farther downward. He stood proudly, excited by her appraisal, enjoying the lingering caress of her eyes.

"Ravenous," she murmured. "You know what an appetite I have."

His smile deepened as he reached for her. "I've got some idea, but there's no harm reminding me."

She blushed, which he thought delightful. A light fragrance clung to her, which he thought came from the cream she had rubbed over her body after showering. As he took her in his arms, the towel felt rough against his chest. He put his hand on the corner she had tucked between her breasts and tugged gently. It clung for a moment around her hips before slipping to the floor where it lay, forgotten.

She stood with her head back, watching him as he looked at her. His breath quickened at the sight of her breasts, high and firm, the nipples already hardened. He touched one lightly, pleased to feel her quiver.

"Are you cold?" he asked. The air-conditioning was on, but not so high as to make the room more than merely comfortable.

She shook her head. "I don't think so."

"Just wondering."

"You don't have to. You already know."

He nodded as his arm went around her waist. Surely no skin could be smoother or softer than hers. Surely no woman could melt so readily, at least not for him. She was boundless and complete in her giving, which brought out the best in him.

"I want," he said as he bent slightly and slipped an arm under her knees, "to know you as completely as I did a few hours ago, but to do it again and again. It's impossible for me to imagine ever having enough of you."

Jo's throat was tight. She could feel her heart pounding and knew that it would be useless to try to speak. What good were words anyway? Touch was so much more effective.

She smiled as he lifted her high against his chest and carried her back to the bed. Her eyes were slumberous as he laid her against the cool sheet, and her arms were welcoming as she opened them to him.

The phone was ringing when David got back to his room. He had left Jo briefly so that he could shower and change before they went down to breakfast. He knew if he had stayed where he was, they would never have gotten out of the room.

He closed the door behind him and reached for the phone on the table beside the undisturbed bed. The voice on the line was a colleague of his at the network, and he was calling with the information David had asked for.

He jotted down the name at the phone company, thanked the man and depressed the receiver. A moment later he was punching in the newly acquired phone number. Five minutes after that he had Martha James's address.

He sat for a short time on the edge of the bed, looking at the notation he had made on the pad. He had a choice of going over there directly or trying again to call her. When she still hadn't answered by the sixth ring, he gave up. All he could hope was that she would be at home.

When he emerged from a quick, cold shower, he glanced at the door connecting his room to Jo's. For the merest instant, he considered going on by himself. As quickly as the thought occurred, he brushed it aside. Any such misguided effort to spare her would be the worst sort of betrayal. Whatever Martha James had to say, Jo had a right to hear it, too.

He dressed in jeans and a blue work shirt that had been softened by innumerable washings. The clothes suited him not only because they were comfortable, but because they didn't shriek out what his profession was. In them, he could blend into the vast mass of other people who might think he looked familiar without being able to place him. This was true no matter how often his face was seen on the nightly news. Being out of context, and not looking as people expected, was often the best disguise available.

When he was ready, he knocked on the door. Jo answered it immediately. She had put on a wrap-around skirt in pale yellow and a matching shirt with slender straps that left her arms bare. Her hair tumbled around a face which, on close examination, looked strained.

"Any luck?" she asked.

He nodded. "I've got the address. All set?"

She hesitated, then nodded. "Sure. Let's go."

They took the rental car, after checking at the desk for directions. Martha James lived on the outskirts of town, as far away from the glitter and glitz as it was possible to get while still being in Las Vegas. Her home was in a mobile trailer park surrounded by a metal fence with an open gate. A sign on the gate warned that it was closed at night.

Most of the trailers seemed to have long since given up any pretext of mobility. They were set on cinder blocks and surrounded by window boxes and small flower beds. Folding lounge chairs were set up here and there, and aluminum awnings were unrolled over many of the windows. Children ran about, busy at their own games and ignoring the adults. Jo and David parked in the area set aside for guests and walked the short distance to Martha James's slot.

There was no one out in front, the blinds were down, and unlike many of the other trailers, the door was firmly closed. Only a faint hum from inside indicated that a fan was running.

"I hope this isn't going to turn out to be a wild-goose chase," David murmured as he approached the door. He knocked once, then again. After several moments when there was still no answer, he came back down the steps to Jo. "Looks as though we may have a problem."

"Let's find out," she said.

Two trailers down, an old man was out in front weeding a flower bed. Jo had noticed him watching them earlier, but as they approached he had his back studiously turned in their direction as he bent over his work.

"Excuse me," Jo said.

He straightened up, feigned a look of surprise and smiled. "Something I can do for you folks?"

"We were just wondering if you know where Martha James is," David said. "We're here to see her."

"Friends of hers?"

David hesitated. He didn't blame the old man for being nosy; he probably had few enough opportunities to exercise his curiosity. But he wasn't about to explain what he was doing there. "She's expecting us," he said.

The old man laughed deeply enough for his stringy chest, bare and tanned to the consistency of leather, to begin to shake. "She is, is she? Old Martha's got you down in an appointment book, I suppose. Why, she's probably running around right now getting things tidied up for your visit."

"I gather you don't think so," David said dryly.

The old man shrugged. "Might be, might not. Let's just say Martha isn't known for her hospitality. She keeps to herself."

"Do you have any idea if she's home now?" Jo asked.

"Car's there," he pointed out, not unreasonably. "Guess Martha is, too."

"She didn't answer the door," David said.

"Probably didn't hear you."

David thought of how firmly he had knocked and was puzzled. "She can't be deaf. I've talked with her on the phone."

The old man laughed again. He was clearly finding the conversation very amusing. "No, she ain't deaf. But she sure can shut everything out when she wants to. Come on, maybe I can give you a hand."

He strode purposefully down the line of trailers, then up the two steps to Martha's door. Instead of knocking as David had done, he merely turned the handle. The door opened. "Lock doesn't work," he explained. "The manager here had to break it to get in a couple of months back, and she never bothered getting another. Hold on a second, and I'll take a look inside."

He was back almost as quickly as he'd promised. "She's there all right, but you ain't gonna have an easy time getting any sense out of her."

David sighed. "Drunk?"

"As a skunk. Try pouring some coffee into her. That usually works." With a grin and a wave, the old codger went back to his garden, leaving them to cope as best they could.

Martha James was sprawled on a couch just inside the front door. She wore pedal pushers and a frilly shirt that would have looked incongruous on a woman half her age. Her poorly dyed blond hair was teased into a beehive hairdo reminiscent of the 1960's, and it had been hair sprayed to the consistency of straw. She lay on her back with her mouth open, an empty bottle of strawberry brandy on the floor beside her. She was snoring.

"Oh, Lord," Jo muttered. "Just what I needed."

David shook his head, not so much in disgust as in simple resignation. This wasn't the first time he'd encountered such a scene. In his line of work, he met all sorts of people in all sorts of conditions. He'd long ago learned that even the worst of them had some worth, and just might have some truth to tell. So he couldn't arbitrarily dismiss Martha James, no matter how much he would have liked to.

"Why don't you go wait in the car?" he suggested to Jo. "There's no reason for you to have to put up with this. I'll call you when she's got herself together."

"That could be a week from now, if ever." Unlike David, Jo was disgusted and thoroughly dismayed. So far as she was concerned, any remote credibility that Martha James might have had was gone. She couldn't understand why he wasn't walking out the door.

"Because," David explained patiently when she asked him that question, "drunkard or not, Greeley has still been paying this woman, and I'm going to find out why."

Jo's mouth tightened. The smell of brandy filling the small trailer made her stomach churn, as did the sight of the woman sprawled on the couch. She steeled herself and turned to David. "I'm staying. The sooner she talks, the sooner this will be over."

## Chapter 15

Two pots of coffee later, a bleary-eyed Martha James looked at them across the small kitchen table and frowned. "What day is it?"

David told her. She sighed, less with surprise than with resignation. "Jeez, that was some bender."

"Do you often drink that much, Mrs. James?" he asked quietly.

She blinked, fumbled for the pack of cigarettes on the table and then tried to light a match. When she couldn't manage that, David took the matches from her, struck one and held it out.

She eyed him before leaning forward, trembling slightly, to get the cigarette going. "Thanks," she said after she had taken a long drag. "Been quite a while since a good-looking guy lit one for me."

"We were talking about your drinking," Jo reminded her.

Martha swiveled her head to look at her. She frowned. "No, he was asking. I don't recall saying anything."

"But you're going to, aren't you?" Jo said. She sat on the other side of the table, next to David, but her attention was strictly on the woman across from her. She stared at her steadily as she went on. "You have to explain about that before we go any further."

Martha's blowsy face stiffened. She took another puff and shrugged. "Don't see why I should."

"What my friend here means," David said, "is that there's a question about your credibility."

Martha tried to laugh, ended up coughing. "Lord," she said when she had caught her breath, "you're something. Why don't you come right out and say it? If it weren't for those checks I sent you, you would have hightailed it out of here the second you got a look at me."

"If it weren't for the checks," he corrected her, "I wouldn't be here in the first place. Now, you've hinted that there's a reason for the payments Greeley made that reflects badly on him. Suppose you tell me what it is."

"Not so fast," Martha said. She stood up, with some effort, made her way to the refrigerator and fished out a can of beer. When she had popped it open, she took a long swallow, belched and returned to the table. It apparently didn't occur to her to offer her guests any refreshment, which was just as well since they weren't inclined to join her, anyway.

"What's in it for me?" she demanded.

"Nothing," David said, "unless what you have to say holds up. Then you'll get exactly what you want."

"And what's that, honey cakes?"

The endearment didn't faze him. Expressionlessly he said, "To destroy Greeley."

Martha was silent for a moment. Jo watched her, barely breathing. She hoped the woman would deny it, would claim some noble motive that would show her up for the liar Jo was sure she was. Or perhaps she would demand money. Unlike some reporters, David was known for never paying for information. If that was what Martha James was hoping for, she was out of luck.

She took another swallow of the beer and eyed him over the rim of the can. "You think you're pretty smart, don't you?"

"You tell me. What have you got against Greeley?"

"Aside from the fact that he's a sanctimonious little twerp, nothing."

Jo had to bite her lip to keep from replying. David's warning hand on her knee reminded her that she was there to listen, not to argue with the other woman. And that was only because of very special circumstances.

Normally she knew that he would never have permitted an employee of a man he was investigating to be present at such an interrogation. David had deliberately not told Martha James her identity, not because he wanted to delude her, but because he was certain that if she knew who Jo was, she would clam up in a second.

The only way Jo could prevent the woman from at least sensing that something wasn't quite right was to keep her mouth firmly shut. She resolved again not to be baited and forced herself to sit back with some semblance of calm.

"So you don't like Greeley," David said. "We'll get back to that in a minute. First, you do drink a lot, don't you?"

"What're you doing, working for Alcoholics Anonymous on the side? Sure I drink. Who doesn't? That's got nothing to do with what I got to say." A note of belligerence had entered the older woman's voice, and she glared at David, as though daring him to challenge her further.

He didn't comment one way or the other, but merely waited for her to continue. After the silence had dragged out for several moments, she did so. "You might say Greeley's got something to do with my drinking. Him and that self-righteous bimbo he married."

She widened her eyes and pretended to smile as her voice took on a singsong note. "Dear, sweet Marianne. Such a pretty girl and so smart. Look at the husband she snagged for herself when she went away to college on that scholarship. Didn't take her any time at all to land him, but then that was no surprise. And now there's people saying she's going to be First Lady. Can you imagine that? If they knew what she used to be like, decent people wouldn't have anything to do with either of them."

"Is that why he was paying you," David asked, "because you've got something on his wife?" He and Jo exchanged a quick glance. Martha had confirmed their earlier guess that Greeley was only vulnerable through his family. It might have come as a relief to Jo that the senator himself wasn't the focus of Martha's vitriol, but it did not. In the final analysis, Jason would do whatever he had to in order to protect those he loved.

"Got something?" Martha repeated with another hoarse laugh. "Yeah, I guess you could put it that way. When a woman sets out to ruin a perfectly decent man, makes him do things that go against his whole nature and then tries to make him take the blame, that's something, isn't it?"

"You'll have to be more specific, Mrs. James," David said. He was speaking automatically while his mind clicked away, assessing what he was hearing. He didn't like this. Not that he expected to be enjoying himself, but usually he was neutral about the information he gathered, at least until he had a chance to check and double-check it. Even then, he tried to keep all emotion out of his reports and usually succeeded.

Just the facts. That creed had been drummed into him from the time he first started as a stringer for a Delaware weekly when he was fifteen. It had carried over to his career in television, staying with him all the way to the top. He privately suspected that a great deal of his success had to do not so much with the magnitude of the stories he covered as with the public's perception of him as a source of straight, unvarnished facts. He had no intention of changing that now or ever.

But the facts or not, he didn't like it. On the surface, Martha James's story seemed straightforward enough, at least so far. She was accusing Marianne Greeley of having had an affair with some man she characterized as decent, a man she claimed had been led by Marianne to do things he wouldn't otherwise have done. That last part was hard to swallow, but it didn't really matter. If Greeley had been paying blackmail money to keep his wife's infidelity from becoming known, his political career was over.

Jo realized that, too. The knot in her stomach was becoming unbearable. She thought of the gracious woman she knew, the devoted wife and mother, and she wanted to shout a denial against such slurs. Only the knowledge that anyone, no matter how fundamentally decent, could slip kept her silent. That and the still stalwart hope that Martha was lying.

"You don't believe me, do you?" the older woman demanded, looking straight at Jo. "Your cute little nose turns up at the mere thought."

Jo kept her tone as steady as she could. "I'm merely wondering how you happen to know all this, or claim to know."

"Because," Martha said promptly, "the man was my husband. We split up ten years ago, and I've got no idea where he is now. But I've got Greeley's checks, and I've got copies of the letters I wrote to him saying I wanted something for what she did to Sam or else I was going to talk. That about clinches it, doesn't it?"

"Not completely," David said. "In a court of law, copies wouldn't be admitted as evidence."

"What the hell does that mean?" Martha demanded, abruptly belligerent again. She slammed her hand down on the table so that the beer can jumped and skittered across it.

Jo grabbed it before it could hit the floor and set the can carefully back on the table. As she did so, she noticed that her hand was trembling.

"Ordinary people aren't gonna care about anything like that. They'll hear what I'm saying, and they'll make up their own minds. Greeley will be cooked."

"Yes," David acknowledged, "he will be." His comment about the inadmissibility of the evidence she offered had merely been a lure, cast out to see how she would react. The way she did left him with no doubt that one way or another, Martha James intended to get her story heard.

"You say you and your husband, Sam, split up ten years ago. That's when you contacted the senator?"

"That's right. Me and Sam were married a real long time and he took real good care of me, let me tell you. I missed that paycheck of his something terrible when he pulled out. So I got to thinking how I could make me a little something, and the senator's name just kind of popped into my mind."

"I can imagine," David murmured. What the hell had Greeley been thinking of to accede to such a demand? The idea of his wife being involved with anyone Martha James might also have known was so incongruous that he could barely consider it seriously. Yet the senator had apparently done so, and in the process gotten himself into some very hot water, indeed.

"All right," David went on, "let's presume for a moment that what you're telling me is correct. I'll need details from you about when this alleged affair between Marianne Greeley and Sam took place. How they met, how long it lasted and so on."

Before she could answer, Jo stood up. She wiped her damp palms on her skirt and took a deep breath. It was very hot in the trailer despite the fan, which whirred fitfully in one corner.

David felt the tension coiling in Jo. He drew back, waiting to see what she would do.

In a voice that sounded very little like her own, Jo asked, "How old was she, Mrs. James?"

The other woman jerked slightly. "What?"

"You heard me. Jason and Marianne Greeley have been married for twenty-five years. In all that time, there's never been a hint of scandal attached to them. Yet you're telling us that at some time in her life, Marianne had an affair with your husband. So I'm asking you, how old was she when that happened?"

Martha hesitated. She looked at David, glancing away hastily when she saw his shuttered gaze. After what seemed like a very long time, she shrugged. "What difference does it make? Some girls mature earlier than others, everybody knows that. She took advantage of it."

Jo walked back to the table and braced her hands on it. She leaned over and looked directly into Martha James's bloodshot eyes. "How old?" she demanded.

A look of fear flashed across the ruined face, followed hard by defiance. She grabbed hold of the beer can, found that it was empty and with a sudden movement, crushed it under her hand. As the metal collapsed, she said, "Twelve. The little whore was twelve at the time."

Jo stood outside the trailer, leaning against the wall. She knew that she should walk back to the car, get in and turn on the air-conditioning. David had given her the keys when he sent her out of the trailer precisely so that she could do that. She clutched them in her hand, thinking of the coolness only a short walk away. But she couldn't get her legs to move.

The old man was still out in front, working on his garden. He looked at her curiously, but she refused to meet his gaze. Instead she forced herself to move, one step at a time, until she finally reached the car.

Once there she slumped behind the wheel, her hand fumbling with the key. Only after the third attempt did she manage to get the engine started and the air conditioner turned on.

For a while, standing outside the trailer in the broiling sun, she had been seriously afraid that she was going to be sick. But that feeling was easing as the cool air enveloped her. She laid her head back against the seat but left her eyes open, staring at the roof of the car without seeing it.

She had no idea what David was saying to Martha James and she didn't want to know. So far as she was concerned, the whole sordid business was over and done with. She only regretted that she was left with knowledge she should not have had.

Her heart went out to Marianne Greeley. When she contrasted what Marianne must have experienced to her own loving and protected childhood, she felt sick all over again. It was hardly news to her that such things happened, but she had never before personally known anyone who had lived through it.

Or at least, she wasn't aware of it if she had. A shroud of secrecy hid such incidents, too often maintained as much by the victim as by the perpetrator. If the statistics were right, she probably knew at least several people who were victims of child abuse. They simply never spoke of it.

That Martha James had actually benefited from the crime against Marianne offended her deeply, yet she could understand that, too. Jason had undoubtedly been buying the other woman's silence on his wife's behalf. Marianne's privacy was very important to her, particularly given how it had been violated in her childhood.

A rap on the car window drew her out of her troubled thoughts. David pointed to the handle on the passenger side. Only then did Jo realize that when she got into the car, she had locked the doors. Instinctively she had wanted to shield herself as much as possible from what lay outside.

She reached across and turned the handle. As he got in and the air-conditioning hit him, he breathed a long sigh of relief. "Do you mind driving?" he asked.

"No, of course not." She started up the car and headed for the gate. They were silent until they reached the main road and started heading toward downtown. As she pressed a little harder on the accelerator, she asked, "When can we get out of here?"

"There ought to be a flight this afternoon. I'll check as soon as we get to the hotel."

Jo nodded. Her hands gripped the steering wheel tightly, but she was already beginning to feel better. Simply getting away from the trailer park had accomplished that much. Nonetheless she was anxious to get out of Las Vegas altogether.

"While you're doing that," she said, "I'll call the senator and tell him the matter's over and done with."

David turned his head and looked at her. Glancing at him out of the corner of her eye, she saw that he appeared very strained and presumed that, like her, he had simply found the experience extremely distasteful.

Not until he spoke did it even occur to her that there might be another problem. "The matter? Is that what you call it?"

"Do you really want me to describe that disgusting, loathsome business in some less neutral term?"

A touch ruefully, he said, "You're doing a good job of that without even trying." More gently, he added, "I realize this is very hard on you, Jo. It is for me, too. But it won't get any easier by our simply refusing to deal with it."

"What are you talking about? It's all over with ... isn't it?"

He hesitated a moment, then sighed deeply. "No, it isn't. We both wish it was, that's clear. But the situation really hasn't changed that much except now I know why Greeley was making the payments."

"I don't believe this," Jo said. She was having difficulty keeping her eyes on the road and was grateful that there was relatively little traffic. "You can't seriously be saying that you still think there is a story."

"It isn't a question of what I think," he said quietly. "There is a story, like it or not. The Greeleys have to deal with that. So do we."

Jo shook her head in bewilderment. She couldn't believe what she was hearing. "You couldn't go on the air with this. I simply can't conceive of that."

"If I don't do it, somebody else will."

"That's your excuse? You might as well go ahead and get the glory because it's going to come out anyway?"

A dark flush spread over David's cheeks, born not of embarrassment but of anger. He was trying hard to see her side and be patient with it, but he felt she was treating him very unfairly and couldn't help but be annoyed by it.

"What glory?" he demanded. "You don't actually believe that I want to tell this story, do you?"

She stomped on the brake to avoid a bus up ahead, swerved into the next lane and hit the accelerator again, all without giving the slightest thought to what she was doing. "I'm definitely getting that impression."

"Well, you're wrong. I'd like nothing better than to walk away from this, but all that means is that somebody else will tell it. Whether you agree or not, I happen to believe that I can do it with more regard for the Greeleys' feelings than they're otherwise likely to get."

"Bully for you," Jo muttered. "You and your whole damn profession. Vultures, that's what you are, feeding on the tragedies and disasters of other people's lives. Don't you have any compassion at all?"

He muttered a low, explicit curse and reached over to steady the wheel. "For God's sake, if you're going to drive, do it, and don't go off the deep end at the same time."

Jo's mouth set in a hard line. He was right, of course, which made it worse. She was so upset by his attitude that she was driving if not recklessly, at least carelessly, and that couldn't go on. Any further discussion would have to be postponed until they reached their hotel.

## Chapter 16

As it happened, they didn't talk again before leaving Las Vegas. Upon arriving at the hotel, both went directly to their rooms. David started to say something as Jo was opening her door, thought better of it and moved on. She went inside, closed the door sharply and told herself that there wasn't anything he could have said that would have made her feel at all different.

The news that he was continuing with the story horrified her, not only for the sake of the Greeleys, but also because it made her wonder if she had understood anything at all about him. She had imagined him to be a tender and sensitive man, strong, intelligent, capable of both giving and receiving love. But she simply could not conceive of such a man doing what he seemed obviously intent on. To expose the suffering of another person, suffering she had clearly struggled desperately to conceal, seemed so callous as to be actually cruel.

She paced back and forth, absently pulling clothes from the closet and stuffing them into her suitcase. All the while she kept glancing at the phone. She had to call the senator, that much she knew, but for the life of her she couldn't imagine what she was going to say.

Finally she forced herself to sit down on the edge of the bed and dial the number she had found on her printed copy of the campaign schedule. It was un-likely that she would be able to reach Jason directly; he would be out on the hustings somewhere. But at least she could let him know that she was returning to Washington, where the current campaign swing was due to wind up the following day.

As she had expected, the senator was not available, but Harry Morton was and he promptly got on the phone.

"Where the hell have you been?" he demanded in a voice so loud that she instinctively held the receiver away from her ear. "Far as that goes, where *are* you? All I got out of Jason was that you went off on some job for him. I've been going out of my mind trying to figure out what's happening."

"It's okay, Harry," she said soothingly, even though she thought it was anything but. "I'm just checking in, that's all. Would you let the senator know that I'll be in the office tomorrow when he is?"

"Hold on. I'm not playing messenger boy for you, sweetheart. Something's up, and I want to know what it is."

Jo was silent for a moment. She could sympathize with Harry who undoubtedly was wondering if his carefully constructed campaign was about to self-destruct, but she wasn't about to tell him anything. Finally she said, "It's a private matter, Harry. I'm sorry, but that's all I can tell you."

"Is Wilson there with you?"

Again she hesitated, weighing what to say. Harry must have noticed that they were both missing. It seemed pointless to deny that they were together. "Yes, he's here."

"Damn it, I knew he had to be behind this. He's got something, doesn't he? How bad is it?"

"Harry, I'm not going to—"

"I don't want the details, for God's sake! They never make any difference in the end. All I want to know is can we ride this out?"

Slowly Jo said, "I don't know."

"What's that supposed to mean?"

"Just what I said. I don't know what's going to happen. It depends on what David—Mr. Wilson—decides to do."

"What's to decide?" Harry demanded. "He's got something, he's going on the air with it. That's how these things work."

"I'm still hoping he won't, although I have to admit it doesn't look good."

Harry gave a low, inarticulate groan. Jo could picture him seated at a battered desk in some regional campaign headquarters, having shooed everybody else out of the room so he could take the call in private. The last time she'd seen him, he had looked tired, frazzled and ready to jump at the slightest sign of trouble. All typical preconvention behavior. He'd be much the same right before the election; they all would be. If they ever got that far.

"I knew he was too good to be true," Harry said. "Greeley had everything going for him, absolutely everything. We were headed for a win, kid. I'll tell you that right now. We would have won big."

"Stop it, Harry," Jo demanded. "Stop talking about him and this campaign in the past tense. We are still very much alive, and we are still going to win."

"Oh, yeah? What're you planning to do, ice Wilson?"

"Believe me," Jo muttered. "If I could put him on ice between now and November, I would. He is the most infuriating man I've ever met. Bone-deep stubborn and so dense you can't even talk to him. How I ever thought that he was attrac—" She broke off abruptly, but not before Harry gave a deep if sorrowful chuckle.

"That how it is, kid? Too bad. Politics doesn't just make for strange bedfellows. Lots of times it makes for no bedfellows at all. At least not when you're talking about a nice girl like you mixing it up with somebody from the media. Those guys will stop at nothing, I mean *nothing* to get what they want. They've got only one thing in mind—get the story. That's their lives, kid, that's what they live for."

Jo took a deep, shaky breath. She was very much afraid that Harry was right. David had suddenly revealed a side of his nature she had never before seen, much less coped with. She had to face the possibility that she had been wrong about him. It wasn't unheard of for a woman to see a man the way she wanted him to be, rather than as he really was. If she had made that mistake, she was going to be paying for it for a very long time.

No, something in her mind said, there's been no mistake. David really is the way you think. You haven't given him a chance to explain why he said what he did about going on with the story.

There is no explanation, another voice said. Except that he obviously deserves his reputation for ruthlessness. No wonder every politician in America is terrified of him. They know that they won't have a secret left by the time he's through.

Wait, the first voice said. Stop jumping to conclusions. Give him a chance.

Cut your losses, the second insisted. You've already made enough of a fool of yourself. Why get hurt even more?

"Harry," Jo murmured, "have you ever had one of those days when you absolutely did not know which way to turn?"

"Every day, sweetie. It goes with the territory. Whenever there's a whole lot of power up for grabs, you can bet there's also going to be a whole lot of flak. Some people are going to get hurt. But I gotta tell you, I'll be genuinely sorry if you turn out to be one of them."

"Thanks," Jo said softly, realizing that he was being sincere. Harry might be a bullheaded throwback to another era, but he could also on occasion be a very nice man. He just didn't like too many people to know it.

"Hang in there, kid," he said. "One way or another, it all comes out in the wash."

Jo hung up a short time later. She sat for a while staring at the phone and trying to get her thoughts in order. They refused to cooperate. She remained torn in two opposite directions over David and what he was doing. The solution was obvious. All she had to do was bang on the connecting door and tell him she wanted to talk. It probably wouldn't be easy or pleasant, but eventually they might be able to clear the air.

Might be. That was what stopped her. There was also the very real possibility they would simply end up so far apart that nothing would ever get them back together.

Her mind—not to speak of her heart—stumbled over that. She found herself sitting hunched over on the bed and abruptly straightened up. Whatever happened, she hadn't lived twenty-eight years and accomplished as much as she had to be laid low by an ill-starred love affair. Somehow she would recover, though she wasn't so foolish as to believe that she would ever be the same.

Refusing to try to look too far into the future and second-guess what might or might not happen, she went over to the door and knocked on it. David answered at once. She saw a glimmer of eagerness in his eyes before her own rigidly withdrawn expression made it fade.

"Did you get us a flight?" she asked.

He nodded. "We've got an hour to make it. Okay?"

She was relieved that it was that soon. Gesturing to her bag, she said, "I'm packed."

They left the hotel in strained silence and were on their way to the airport, with David driving this time, before he said, "Did you speak to the senator?"

Jo shook her head. "I didn't expect to be able to reach him at this time of day, but I left a message that we're heading for Washington. I expect he'll call me at home this evening."

"I'd like to be there when he does."

Her eyes flashed. Whatever else David was, no one could accuse him of timidity. "You're asking an awful lot."

"I know. But I need to speak to him as soon as possible. If you prefer, I'll give you the number of my hotel, and you can ask him to call me there."

Jo hesitated. That was the wisest course, but she couldn't bring herself to say so. She kept remembering what Jason had said about it not being a good idea for them to be separated at such a time, and she wondered if David was thinking of that, too.

"Are you sure," she asked, "that you want me to hear whatever you have to say to him?"

David shrugged. "You already know most of it. Moreover Greeley knew what you'd be hearing when he asked you to come along with me. So it's hardly as though I'd be breaching a confidence. Besides, I have the impression it's the only way I'm going to get you to listen to my side."

Jo sighed. She knew he had a point. So far she had been unwilling to accept his rationale for continuing with the story. She had also made some pretty harsh accusations against him. Now that she thought about it, he was dealing with those very calmly.

When she said as much, David managed a faint smile. "I've had worse said to me, though I have to admit that you pack a much bigger wallop than anybody else. I don't like knowing that you think I trade on other people's grief. I guess I'm still hoping to convince you otherwise.''

"I'm sorry I was so harsh," Jo murmured. His candor took her aback. She wasn't sure if she could respond in kind, but she did want to try. "It's just that when I realized you intended going on with the story, I felt so betrayed."

A pulse leaped in his jaw. She had struck a nerve. "That's the last way I want you to feel. But you can't make this a test of loyalty between us. When I fell in love with you, I didn't also sign on to get Greeley elected. That isn't my priority."

Jo barely heard the last sentence. "David," she said softly, "you never use words lightly, do you?"

He cast her a quick, penetrating look. "No, never. I know what I said and I meant it. But," he added with a rueful grin, "this isn't exactly the time or place to discuss it, is it?"

"Not unless we want to drive off the road," she agreed, returning his smile, though warily. He loved her, or at least he said he did, and with David that amounted to the same thing. She should have been ecstatic. Instead she felt only a growing sense of fear that she had come so close to something rare and precious, only to lose it because of a twist of fate.

"Do you remember what you said," she asked, "about wishing that we had met under different circumstances?"

He nodded. "I've been thinking about that. Maybe this isn't such a bad break, after all."

Jo couldn't help but wonder how he had come to that conclusion when she was convinced of exactly the opposite. "Why not?"

"Because we're being forced to deal with a serious problem right at the outset of our relationship. We're either going to make it or..."

He didn't finish the sentence; he didn't have to. She turned and stared out the window, thinking about the situations people got themselves into and where they could lead.

There were only a handful of passengers for the flight to Washington. It seemed that almost no one left Las Vegas in the middle of the week, at least not for the nation's capital. As they took off into the cloudless sky, Jo took one last look at the city sprawled out across the desert and grimaced. Maybe some day she would come back under different circumstances and decide that she liked the place, but she really doubted it. Fairly or not, some places were tainted by their associations. She wouldn't mind if she never returned.

There was a movie on the flight, a comedy that had done well in the theaters the year before. She put on the headphones and tried to watch, but her attention kept wandering. Finally she got up and went to the lavatory where she bathed her face and wrists in cold water. The shimmering heat of Las Vegas seemed to cling to her even at thirty thousand feet. When she looked up at herself in the mirror, her eyes were slightly puffy, as though they had stared at the sun too long.

David gave her a quizzical look as she returned to her seat. "Are you all right?" he asked quietly.

She nodded "Fine, just tired."

A look of tenderness and concern flashed across his face. "This will all be over soon."

She managed a smile that was only slightly bleak. "Not soon enough for me." Unaccountably she shivered.

He had stood up to let her pass since she had the window seat. Now he reached into the overhead bin and found a blanket which he laid over her. When she would have protested, he touched a gentle finger to her lips. "Go to sleep, Jo. Everything will look better when you're rested."

She hadn't intended to do as he said, but her body had other ideas. While the movie continued to flash across the screen, she closed her eyes, only for a few moments, she thought. Before she was aware of what was happening, she drifted off.

David looked at her from beneath hooded eyes. Huddled under the blanket, she seemed fragile and childlike, impressions he knew were erroneous. Jo was a strong, self-reliant woman who was more than capable of standing on her own two feet. That was part of what attracted him so strongly to her.

The thought of losing her was like a knife twisting through him. He could hardly bear it, yet he knew that if the alternative was to compromise himself, he wouldn't be left with much choice. He had long ago accepted that he wasn't the sort of person who could— as the saying went—go along to get along. He'd been called a troublemaker, a muckraker and a few other things that were unprintable by people who didn't understand his refusal to bend his convictions to suit them.

Over the years, he'd been offered some heady inducements. The outright attempts at bribery were the least of it. There was also the subtly seductive promise that his cooperation would earn him access to the highest reaches of power. He knew that there were people in his business who had fallen prey to such blandishments. He didn't so much despise as pity them.

The irony, of course, was that by holding firm to his convictions, he had acquired power himself. Not too long ago, a poll had been taken asking people to name those public figures they trusted most. His name had popped up in the top five. The network executives had been delighted; they saw it as a ratings boost. David saw it as graphic proof of the responsibility he carried.

People believed what he told them was the truth. So it had to be. It was as simple as that, and as unforgiving. He couldn't hedge, fudge or engage in any of the other euphemisms for plain old lying. But he could decide that something simply wasn't news. He'd done it in the past, in situations similar to the one he was in now.

He'd walked away from information he thought didn't properly belong in the public domain and had seen other reporters pick up the story and run with it. That didn't bother him. What did was the cost to innocent people caught up in the glare of publicity that could burn and scar as severely as any flash fire.

He didn't want that to happen to Marianne Greeley. Not because he thought her husband ought to be president—he was reserving his opinion on that—but simply because she was a decent human being who deserved a whole lot better than what she'd get at the hands of certain of his colleagues.

He turned and looked at Jo again. It was incredible to think that they had spent only two nights together. He felt as though he had known her always, yet as though every time he saw her was the first.

He was getting downright poetic. In another moment he'd be remembering love songs and forgetting the problem they faced. As though he could. It loomed ahead of them, growing larger with every mile that the plane crossed. He felt like a man on the edge of a mine field with nowhere to go except straight ahead.

With a sigh, he lifted the armrest that separated them and drew her closer. She murmured softly in her sleep, but didn't wake. With her head nestled on his shoulder, he drew the blanket over them both and laid his cheek against her silken hair. She always smelled so good, like spring air after a rain. Poetic.

His eyelids were growing heavier. He let them close while he shifted her slightly so that she was lying more fully in his arms. She felt so right against him, like a dream he had never known he had until it became reality.

Deep inside him in the most secret recesses of his soul, his resolve hardened. Damn the vagaries of fate—he was not going to lose her. He was going to fight with every means at his disposal and worry about the consequences later.

# Chapter 17

It was raining when they reached Washington. "I don't believe this," Jo muttered as they waited for a cab. She was shivering in the thin clothes she had put on in Las Vegas. Goose bumps appeared on her arms as she stared out at the dripping sky. "We should forget about the election and start building arks."

David laughed gently. He took off his khaki jacket and draped it over her shoulders. She cast him a quick, surprised look. "You'll get cold."

He shook his head. "No, it's all right. I'm fine."

As she reluctantly but gratefully gathered the jacket more snugly around herself, she had to agree that he certainly looked as he claimed. Standing tall and bareheaded, wearing a work shirt and jeans, he appeared perfectly relaxed and confident. When he turned to glance down the road, his profile was hard, chiseled perfection. He spotted a cab and raised his arm, bringing it to a screeching stop.

Once in the back seat, Jo gave the driver the address of her apartment, then glanced at her watch, which she had reset to the correct time as they were landing. It was early evening. With luck, the senator would be calling her in a few hours.

"We shouldn't have long to wait," she murmured as the cab crossed the bridge heading into the city. Traffic was very heavy as was usual at that hour. She settled back in the seat, trying not to think about David beside her. Out of the corner of her eye she could see the long, powerful line of his body so close to her own. He seemed deep in thought, for which she was grateful. The effort of conversation was beyond her.

When they had pulled up in front of her apartment, David paid off the driver as Jo unlocked the front door. He followed her inside with the bags. "I should let my landlord know that I'm home," she said.

Francis answered her knock promptly. He was holding Wilson in his arms. The little kitten glanced at them and yawned.

"It doesn't look as though I've been missed," Jo said with a smile. "Is everything all right?"

He assured her that it was as he looked in David's direction. "I don't believe we've met."

Jo performed the introductions, though they were hardly necessary since both men knew each other by sight and reputation. "I admire your work," Francis said. "Television could use more people like you. But tell me, are you still writing books?"

"I hope to do another," David said, "once the election is over. Right now, it's a bit hard to find the time."

Francis nodded understandingly. He asked if they would care to come in for a drink, but Jo declined for both of them, explaining they had work to do. That prompted a smile from Francis, which left her with the distinct impression that he didn't quite believe her.

"Nice man," David said as they were climbing the steps to her apartment. "He seems like he'd make a good friend."

"He does," Jo confirmed. "By the way, did you know that he and Elizabeth were acquainted at one time?"

David hesitated. As he opened her door, he said, "I'd heard something to that effect, but it was years ago."

"It seems strange that two people who move in the same circles in this city haven't seen each other for so long."

"Not so strange if you take into account that they've been deliberately avoiding each other all that time."

"But why?" Jo asked as she switched on the light. At first glance the apartment looked faintly strange to her, as though she had been away much longer than she actually had. She supposed that was because so much had happened since her hasty departure.

"Haven't you guessed?" David asked. When she shook her head, he said, "If you'll make a pot of coffee, I'll tell you the story. I don't think Elizabeth would mind. She seems to have taken a fancy to you and at any rate, it's hardly a secret."

They left their bags in the living room. David followed her into the kitchen and took a seat at the polished oak table. The kitchen was small but efficiently laid out. It had tiled counters and cabinets fitted with glass panes through which could be seen her collection of Depression-era dishes. The vivid blues, pinks and greens formed a cheery backdrop that was echoed by the curtains fluttering at the single window.

In front of the window was a woven basket filled by a feathery fern. David looked at it pensively as he said, "Elizabeth and Francis were in love at one time, but they were both married to other people to whom they felt a considerable commitment. Nowadays people seem to walk away from marriages so easily that when you hear of one that's lasted, it's an oddity. But back then things were different. Despite his feelings for Elizabeth, Francis genuinely cared for his wife and couldn't bear to hurt her. Elizabeth's relationship with her husband wasn't so clear-cut, but she didn't feel that she could simply walk out. So they parted, hoping I'm sure that they would get over each other."

Jo filled the filter basket with coffee and slid it into place. Softly she said, "But they didn't. Otherwise they wouldn't have bothered to go on avoiding each other all these years."

"You may be right," David agreed. "But I can understand their problem. After so many years, each is probably afraid that the other has forgotten. If one of them made an overture now, there could be even more hurt."

As Jo set the coffee cups on that table, she asked, "Do you think they made a mistake when they stayed in their marriages?"

"Who's to say? They had standards that they believed in, and they lived by them. Maybe if they'd come together despite them, they would have ended up being disillusioned with each other. This way at least they've had a dream to hold on to."

"They were really stuck, weren't they?" Jo said softly. "There was no middle ground for them."

David nodded. "The middle ground is always the hardest to find. In their case, compromise wasn't possible. You can't be true to a marriage and be involved with somebody else at the same time. But even if their situation had been different, if there had been some other conflict, finding a resolution is always difficult."

She looked at him directly across the table, her eyes wide and searching. No matter how many times she saw him, she couldn't seem to get enough. Each time was new, exciting, distinct. She had the sudden conviction that such would always be the case. Had Elizabeth felt the same? How terrible to have been caught between unforgiving ideals and undying love. Terrible and achingly familiar. "Difficult," she murmured.

He reached across the table and took her hand, turning it over so that his thumb could caress the sensitive inner skin of her palm. She jumped slightly and trembled. When she would have pulled back, his grip tightened, not in the least hurtfully but firmly enough for her to give up what had been at best a halfhearted effort.

Instead she let her hand lie in his and allowed the sensations his touch provoked, as she said, "David, I have ideals, too, and one of them is that I respect as well as desire the man I love. It's true that people who work in politics are afraid of you, but that doesn't mean that you aren't also admired. Certainly I've always thought highly of your work. But I have to tell you the truth: if you go on the air and expose Marianne's secret, I simply won't be able to bear it.

"I know," she added hastily before he could speak, "what you're saying about the story coming out one way or another. But if it has to be told, I don't want you to do it. Whoever does is going to be terribly stained by it, at least in my eyes."

He was silent for several moments, then softly he said, "Sometimes I think I can be a really arrogant jerk when I want to."

Her eyes widened. "What are you talking about?"

He shrugged, as though it was obvious. "I have a hard time trusting people. I tend to think that if something's going to be done right, I have to be the one to do it. None of that surprises me, given my background, but it isn't exactly easy to deal with."

"No," Jo said gently, "I imagine it isn't."

"You're different. You know how to trust and how to give. I have to admit that I envy that."

Jo's throat was tight. She knew without having to be told that it was very difficult for him to speak in such a way. He was a man who lived in the external world in all its rough and tumble rather than the internal world of the mind and spirit. He gave his attention to other people rather than to himself.

But for all that, he was hardly ignorant about the legacy of his childhood and what it had done to him. With her, he caught at least a glimpse of a different way. That humbled her even as she accepted the responsibility for helping him to reach it.

"David," she said softly, "when you speak of something being done right, what do you mean in this case?"

"I don't want Marianne hurt," he admitted. "To me the story isn't important. It's just a sordid little episode in the context of the campaign. I'll feel perfectly justified in minimizing it, but that will be enough to drain it of its shock value. Other reporters won't be so quick to pick it up once they feel they've been scooped. For a day or two, people will be talking about it. They'll probably sympathize with the Greeleys, but then they'll go on to other things, and that will be that."

"For everyone except Marianne. She'll have to live with other people knowing. How do you suppose that will make her feel?"

He shook his head sadly. "Jo, I just don't have any other solution."

She hesitated, but only briefly. Having taken a deep breath she proposed the solution that had come into her mind, born of subconscious wrangling of the most desperate sort. "Let her tell it. Trust her at least enough to give her the chance."

He frowned as he considered an alternative which had clearly not occurred to him. "She's been desperate to keep it hidden all these years. How can you imagine that she'll suddenly be able to speak about it?"

"Because she's a strong woman, and she has a man at her side who truly loves her. Jason would give up anything to protect her, I'm sure of that. But she won't let him. If she can't do it for her own sake, she'll do it for his."

"Has it occurred to you that's exactly the sacrifice he doesn't want her to make? I certainly wouldn't. If he bows out of the race now, Martha James's story loses all its impact. Nobody could care less about what an ex-candidate did or why. It's only if he stays in that it matters. What you're proposing could force him to quit rather than let her do it."

"Which is exactly the sacrifice she doesn't want him to make. In fact, I'm willing to bet that she'll do anything to prevent it from happening. Not only that, but she'll do it well, with her head high and her spirit intact."

"You know her that well?" he asked.

"No," Jo admitted, "she's always kept pretty much to herself. I thought it was just what she preferred, now I realize there's more to it. But that doesn't change anything. I'm sure she can deal with this herself. She doesn't need you or Jason to do it for her. Just trust her."

He was reluctant, she could see that clearly, but she could also see that he was thinking about it. With a slight smile, she got up from the table and went to get the coffee. When she returned to fill their cups, he said quietly, "I suppose it's worth a try."

Inwardly she sighed with relief. "It's the middle ground, in between what you think is right and what I think is right."

He grinned a bit crookedly. "And it's slippery as hell."

She could hardly refute that, especially not while she was frantically praying that she was right, that Marianne was as strong as she hoped and that her plan would work.

David saw the doubt in her eyes, and the fear. He reached out and touched her face gently, stroking a finger down the curve of her cheek in a caress that was as comforting as it was arousing.

The gesture worked both ways. He was almost painfully hard as he looked at her. She made him feel like a boy again, hardly able to control his most basic needs. Not only for sex; rather to his surprise, that was turning out to be the least of it. She offered far more: tenderness, understanding, support.

He stood up, smiling down at her as he held out his arms. "You know, beautiful lady, you're addictive."

Her body swayed toward him, drawn by a power she could not resist. "David . . ."

He heard the fear in her voice, the concern that made her want to hold back no matter how difficult that was, and for a moment hesitation gripped him. He was almost tempted to let her go. Almost, but not quite.

Every instinct he possessed reinforced the resolution he had made on the plane. He thought of the times in the orphanage and later in the navy when he'd had to fight for what he wanted, sometimes against unfair odds. He'd always won, not only because as he grew he'd become bigger and tougher and harder than other men, but because he was simply more determined.

That hadn't changed.

He reached down and gently plucked her out of the chair. It always came as a shock to her to be reminded of how strong he was. City men weren't, generally.

Men who sat behind desks tended to be soft. Even if they worked out in health clubs, it wasn't the same as the strength that came from a lifetime of hard, physical work.

Yet David possessed exactly that kind of strength, along with the grace and agility that seemed to come with it naturally. She would have been less than a woman if she hadn't been irresistibly drawn to him. Her mouth curved in a languorous smile as she remembered that first day in her office.

"What are you thinking about?" he asked.

Still smiling, she shook her head. "I can't tell you."

"Why not?"

"Because—" she reached up and ran her hands through his thick golden hair. Her tone changed abruptly, becoming light and teasing. "Because you've already got a big enough head."

He laughed and nuzzled her throat with his lips. The effect was electric, sending a shivering bolt of sheer pleasure through her. "Tell me anyway," he murmured.

"Won't," she gasped. "You can't make me." On a more reasonable note, she added, "However, you're welcome to try."

He raised his head and looked directly at her. "Am I, Jo? Welcome, I mean?"

She was silent for a moment, understanding what he was asking and uncertain as to what to say. This was her chance to draw back. If she did she knew he would never try to insist, no matter how much he wanted her. He was simply far too honorable and decent a man for that. He would accept her decision, however painful it was to him. The responsibility for what happened next rested squarely on her shoulders.

Knowing that did not disturb her. She accepted it as naturally as she accepted the warmth seeping through her body and the accelerated beating of her heart. Choices. Life was full of them. Some tougher than others, but none really easy.

As a child she had debated over whether to have chocolate or strawberry ice cream on the Saturday afternoon trips into town. She had stood in front of the drugstore fountain, tasting anticipation as sweet as the treat itself.

Later on she had made the choice between staying in Oklahoma and becoming what people presumed she would be—and leaving to invent herself according to her own dreams. Up until now, that had been the toughest thing she'd done.

"I feel," she whispered, "as though I'm standing on the very top of a diving platform, and there's no way off except to jump."

David's mouth quirked at the corners. "How good a swimmer are you?"

She met his smile with her own. "Not bad at all."

He gave a low groan deep in his chest and gathered her closer. She felt the hardness of his body pressing against her and gloried in it. Her hands ran over his broad chest as she savored the tensile strength of him. She frowned at the obstacle his shirt presented.

"Don't stop now," he said encouragingly.

"I don't think I could," she murmured as her fingers went to work on the buttons. She was more than a little clumsy, but eventually she managed to get them undone. With a low sigh of sheer pleasure, she slipped her hands beneath the cloth. The first touch of his bare skin sent a bolt of exquisite delight soaring through her. She had to bite her lower lip to keep from crying out.

"Don't hold back, Jo," he murmured huskily. "Do whatever feels right to you."

The freedom he gave her was all but overwhelming. Elated by it, she threw back her head and laughed. Her finely shaped face was framed by the swirling mop of short chestnut curls. Beneath the thin shirt she wore, her nipples were clearly outlined. He glanced down at her, and a dark flush spread over his cheeks.

"Sweet Lord, how beautiful you are."

"So are you," she whispered, her palms tingling as she ran them over him. His skin was smooth and warm. She loved the touch of it, but the taste was even more entrancing. Unhesitantly she bent forward and flicked her tongue over a flat male nipple.

His hands tightened on her arms as a low gasp was wrung from him. Lightly she raked him with her teeth, and the effect was devastating.

With a set jaw, David said, "I have nothing against the idea, you understand, but unless you want to be taken on the kitchen floor, I suggest we adjourn to the bedroom."

Jo never quite remembered getting there. Somehow they made their way down the hall, trailing bits of clothes behind them. His shirt fell by the wayside, as did her own. Their shoes were discarded along with her skirt. By the time they reached the bedroom, he wore only his jeans and she was clad only in lacy fragments of lingerie.

His smile was almost wolfish as he surveyed her. She looked slender and firm in the pale light filtering through the curtains that shaded the high windows. It was an old-fashioned room, large and spacious with a tall ceiling that still boasted its original molding. In it Jo had placed a large Victorian sleigh bed, found at a barn sale before such things became fashionable. She had refinished it herself, and the dark, rich wood gleamed. It was made up with lacy sheets in pale ivory, a matching comforter and heaps of lace-covered pillows.

David had already decided that he was crazy about that bed. Given an option, he would never rest his head anywhere else, although just then resting wasn't what was on his mind.

His big hands shook slightly as he reached behind her slender back and undid the clasp of her bra. It fell forward and she shrugged it off. He sucked in his breath and he cupped her breasts, catching the nipples between his thumbs and forefingers.

"What you do to me," she whispered on a note of awe.

"And you to me." Gently he took her hand and pressed it against him, letting her feel the full extent of his need for her. Her fingers lingered, stroking him, until he groaned with pleasure. The zipper of his jeans rasped softly as he pushed it down, freeing him further. "Jo . . ." he murmured thickly.

"Let me," she said as she took him in both hands, savoring the power and heat of him. With a sense of wonder, she felt him tremble in response. His jeans fell to the floor and he stepped out of them, wordlessly removing his one remaining garment as he did so.

He stood before her naked, allowing her free rein to indulge her most sensual desires, until his control was on the brink of shattering. Only then did he pull her away and urgently draw her to the bed.

She gasped when he slipped the lacy panties from her, then gently slid his hands between her thighs, stroking and caressing until she cried out. When she tried to reach for him, he eluded her, holding her wrists to the bed and settling his body between her legs so that she couldn't resist him.

Her back arched like a tautly drawn bow. She cried out again, almost sobbing with the force of the pleasure he gave her. "No more, David, please!"

He let go of her wrists and came over her, slipping a hand beneath her buttocks to lift her to him. "Much more," he murmured tightly. "Much, much more. A lifetime's worth."

He slipped into her with ease and power, claiming her as his own even as she claimed him. Their bodies rose and fell together, slick and gleaming in the slowly darkening shadows.

Outside, the rain fell more heavily. Thunder rolled off toward the north beyond the city. A finger of lightning split the sky. A clean, cool scent freshened the air blowing in past the lace curtains. It washed over the heated bodies entwined on the bed, caressing them as they caressed one another, dissolving barriers and boundaries and setting in their place the foundation for the future to come.

# Epilogue

Sweating under the glare of the television lights suspended above the speaker's platform, the party secretary leaned into the microphone.

*"Al-a-ba-ma!"*

A portly gentleman on the convention floor rose as the other members of his delegation hoisted their banners and cheered. When the tumult died down slightly, he said, "Madame Secretary, the great state of Alabama is privileged to cast all votes for the next president of the United States, Jason Greeley!"

Cheers erupted throughout the convention hall. They continued unabated for several minutes until the rapping of the gavel finally restored something close to order, if it could be called that. A good-natured exuberance had seized the convention sometime around the second day when most of the party infighting came to its inevitable conclusions, and people got down to the serious business of picking a candidate.

*"A-las-ka!"*

A grinning young man fought his way to the microphone set up in front of that delegation. "Madame Secretary, the great *and* glorious state of Alaska, last frontier of this magnificent nation, is privileged to join our sister state of Alabama in casting all votes for the next president of the United States, Jason Greeley!"

Jo leaned back against the couch and watched the scene before her. She was staring at a bank of three televisions, one for each of the major networks, set up in the living room of Jason Greeley's hotel suite. He was staying a discreet distance from the convention hall. As tradition dictated, he wouldn't actually appear there until he had received his party's nomination.

At the moment he was comfortably ensconced in an armchair next to the couch, his shirt undone and his feet propped up on an ottoman. He had a can of beer in his hand, from which he took occasional sips. Outside, beyond the suite, the media was being held at bay. They would be admitted after the final tally was done, not before.

*"Ar-i-zona!"*

As the camera switched to the chairman of that state's delegation, Harry Morton said, "New York'll put you over the top."

Jason smiled slightly. "You're sure about that, Harry?"

The campaign manager gave him a chiding glance. "Would I set it up any other way? It's all fixed. New

Mexico's gonna pass. It's only right your home state gets to do it.''

Jason shook his head ruefully. ''What does New Mexico get in return for the courtesy?''

Harry spread his hands. ''So you'll owe them a couple of drop-ins the next time there's a local election. Big deal. Presidents have to do that kind of thing all the time anyway.''

Arizona had proudly cast all its votes for Greeley, too. Jo checked them off on the clipboard she held on her lap and grinned at Harry. ''You're feeling confident these days.''

He shrugged and glanced out the window. They were on the fifteenth floor of the hotel, but even from there they could see the crowd gathered out in front. Jason Greeley didn't go anywhere now without such a crowd forming. People wanted to see and hear him, even simply to be close to him. Touching, of course, was out of the question. The Secret Service saw to that.

There was even an agent in the room with them. He was a big, rumpled man with watchful eyes and a no-nonsense manner. So far, there had been no need for him or any of his colleagues to prove their skill at protecting Jason. Jo could only pray there never would be.

He was going to win. Sitting there in the hotel, watching as his party went through the process of naming him their candidate, she knew that. It wasn't simply a matter of believing or hoping. She was rock-solid sure of it in a way she couldn't quite explain but couldn't shake, either.

The fact that he was fifteen points ahead in the polls against the other party's nominee went a long way toward convincing her. True, there were several months of hard, intensive campaigning before the election, but Jason had already passed through his hardest time of testing. He was on the home stretch, and she knew it.

Beside him, Marianne reached over to touch his hand and smile. They shared a private moment in the midst of the tumult that Jo couldn't help but envy. There had been few enough for them in the months immediately preceding the convention. When Marianne wasn't campaigning at her husband's side, she was off on her own, speaking to audiences that were as glad to see her as they would have been to have Jason himself. She handled such occasions with grace and dignity and had even confessed to Jo that she was beginning to enjoy it.

*"Ar-kan-sas!"*

Harry bounced up and down on the balls of his feet. He was trying hard to conceal his nervous energy, without great success. Left to himself, he would have been down there right now on the convention floor, wheeling and dealing until the last possible moment.

Jason had specifically forbidden him to do so, saying that it was now up to the delegates to make up their own minds. Harry had groaned at that and held his head, but he hadn't really tried very hard to get Jason to reconsider. He knew, as they all did, that nobody was going to beat them now.

"Got the speech ready?" he asked Jo.

She nodded, pointing to a sheaf of papers on the nearby table. "Ready, set, go."

"It's a good one, Jo," Jason said. "I couldn't have asked for better."

"I should hope not," she said with a grin, "since you wrote most of it." They had stayed up late the night before, working on his acceptance speech. It was a source of pride to her that she'd made some contributions to it, but she wasn't misstating the case when she said that most of it had come directly from Jason himself. She was looking forward to hearing him deliver it.

Which, judging by the way things were going, would be soon.

*"California!"*

Jason took a last swallow of his beer and tossed the can in the trash basket. He looked at his wife and smiled. "I've got a feeling it's too late to reconsider."

She laughed, looking very young and very happy. But then Jo thought Marianne Greeley had been looking that way since shortly after the day she had stood up in front of microphones and cameras to announce her sponsorship of an agency to prevent child abuse. She had mentioned in passing that she had been a victim of such abuse herself and that she was determined to do everything possible to wipe it out.

Yes, there had been headlines, but only for a day or two. Exactly as David had predicted, when robbed of its shock value the story died away quickly. The agency, however, would not. Marianne was sincere in her resolution to work to protect children from a crime whose effects she knew only too well.

Surprisingly to Jo, although less so upon reflection, Marianne had jumped at the suggestion that she be the one to reveal what had happened to her. Her only concern was whether or not she would be able to do it properly. David had put aside his impartial stance in order to coach her for her appearance before the television cameras.

The advice he had given her—to relax and simply say what was in her heart—had worked perfectly. Jo had no doubt that forever after people would think of Marianne as a lady of unusual courage and strength. That had more than a little to do with the widespread support her husband was receiving.

"The voters elect the First Lady as much as they do the president," Francis MacInnes had said on an evening shortly before the convention when Jo stole a few hours to have dinner with him and Elizabeth. The companionship that was growing up between those two warmed her deeply. She basked in its glow even as she wished that David could have joined them.

"It will be over soon," Elizabeth had said with an understanding smile.

Jo was counting on that. She knew exactly how many days remained to the election and how many days there were between then and the inauguration. She intended making the best possible use of all of them.

*"New York!"*

A bit guiltily, she wrenched herself back from her reverie, not particularly surprised to discover that she had kept a steady count of the votes even while her mind wandered. As Harry had promised, New York was in position to put its favorite son over the top.

"Madame Secretary," the delegation chairman boomed, "the great state of New York—the Empire State—duly mindful of the great honor done to it, with a humble spirit and hopeful heart, casts all votes for that good and trustworthy man, *President* Jason Greeley!''

Bands played, whistles blew and banners were hoisted. Across the television screens, the panoply of American politics exploded in all its boisterous vitality. It would be some time before the din died down enough for the chairman to propose that the convention complete its voting through acclamation and make the nomination unanimous.

In the meantime, Jason Greeley stood to receive the embrace of his wife and the congratulations of his staff. Then he went into the bedroom for a few private moments with Marianne before they left for the convention hall.

Jo gathered up her papers and prepared to leave the suite. The voting might be virtually over, but there was still a great deal she had to do. Before she left, however, she glanced back over her shoulder at the television screens.

On one of them, the young anchor, Judith Fairchild, was summing up what had just occurred. From her booth above the convention floor, she said, ''No one could say this was a surprise, David, could they? Jason Greeley's nomination was pretty much a foregone conclusion before this convention opened. Isn't that right?''

The camera switched to David. Jo felt the familiar quickening in her blood that came whenever she saw him. She smiled ruefully, knowing that it would always be that way with her.

''He won the nomination on the hustings,'' David confirmed. ''The convention simply ratified that.''

"What would you say about his prospects in the election?" Judith inquired.

David smiled. "The polls speak for themselves, though every politician worth his salt will claim not to believe in them. I'm sure Greeley isn't taking anything for granted, but his election won't be any more of a surprise than what's just happened here today."

"Thanks, David. We're going to take a break now and go to our sponsors. We'll be back with further coverage of the convention directly."

Jo turned to go. Outside in the hallway, she saw the press gathering and knew they wouldn't be held back much longer. Not that they should be. The people had a right to see and hear the candidate as much as possible. She fielded several questions herself as she made her way to the elevators.

No, she didn't know exactly when the senator would reach the convention, but it would be soon. No, it wasn't true that she had already accepted a position in the Greeley administration. That would have been premature. There would be plenty of time to discuss such things after the election.

Time for other things, too. A staff car gave her a ride to the convention hall. Once there, she sidestepped the swirling, shouting mass of delegates and made her way to a quiet room toward the back. It was furnished with metal desks and chairs, a coffee machine and a table with boxes of Danishes and sandwiches. The room was typical of press rooms everywhere.

David was leaning against a wall. He looked up as she entered and a slow, provocative smile lit his eyes. Jo returned it as a rush of warmth spread over her.

"How's the candidate?" he asked.

She laughed. "Typical reporter, think of the story first. Good thing I'm thick-skinned."

"No, you aren't," he said softly, running a hand up her bare arm so that she shivered.

"Stop that," she murmured, halfheartedly. There was no one else in the press room at the moment, but that could change.

He ignored her protest and bent to kiss her long and lingeringly. When he raised his head, the light burning in his eyes told her they were of the same mind.

"Sometimes," she murmured, "I think I've really learned to hate this campaign. It keeps getting in the way of far more interesting pursuits."

"We've managed," he reminded her with a look that made her blush. Actually, they'd managed quite well, finding time to be together whenever they could throughout the past few months. It would continue to be difficult for a while, but once the election was over...

"I need to speak with Greeley sometime soon," David said.

"You know he's always glad to see you."

"Good, then he shouldn't have any objection when I ask him to take a day off after the election to be our best man."

Jo glanced down at the diamond gleaming on her finger and nodded. She had the feeling that Jason was looking forward to performing that service for them. He had, after all, brought them together.

Or was it more correct to say that fate had simply done that? Down below on the convention floor the band was playing "God Bless America." History was being made in a very public, dramatic fashion. Beyond the election itself, it was impossible to say exactly what would happen. There would be problems, certainly, and crises, but Jo felt every confidence that they would be dealt with well and fairly.

She looked at the man she loved, the man beside whom she was destined to live, and she knew a sense of such complete rightness that for a moment it blocked out everything else.

Then the door burst open, the world tumbled in, and they walked out into it, together.

\* \* \* \* \*

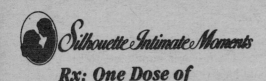

## Silhouette Intimate Moments

### Rx: One Dose of

> # DODD MEMORIAL HOSPITAL

In sickness and in health the employees of Dodd Memorial Hospital stick together, sharing triumphs and defeats, and sometimes their hearts as well. Revisit these special people next month in the newest book in Lucy Hamilton's Dodd Memorial Hospital Trilogy, *After Midnight*—IM #237, the time when romance begins.

Thea Stevens knew there was no room for a man in her life—she had a young daughter to care for and a demanding new job as the hospital's media coordinator. But then Luke Adams walked through the door, and everything changed. She had never met a man like him before—handsome enough to be the movie star he was, yet thoughtful, considerate and absolutely determined to get the one thing he wanted—Thea.

Finish the trilogy in July with *Heartbeats*—IM #245.

To order the first book in the Dodd Memorial Hospital Trilogy, *Under Suspicion*—IM #229 Send your name, address and zip or postal code, along with a check or money order for $2.75 for each book ordered, plus 75¢ postage and handling, payable to Silhouette Reader Service to:

| In Canada | In U.S.A. |
|---|---|
| P.O. Box 609 | 901 Fuhrmann Blvd. |
| Fort Erie, Ontario | P.O. Box 1396 |
| L2A 5X3 | Buffalo, NY 14269-1396 |

Please specify book title with your order.

# ATTRACTIVE, SPACE SAVING BOOK RACK

Display your most prized novels on this handsome and sturdy book rack. The hand-rubbed walnut finish will blend into your library decor with quiet elegance, providing a practical organizer for your favorite hard-or soft-covered books.

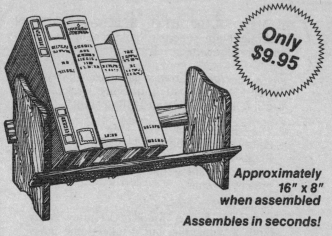

**Only $9.95**

**Approximately 16" x 8" when assembled**

**Assembles in seconds!**

---

To order, rush your name, address and zip code, along with a check or money order for $10.70* ($9.95 plus 75¢ postage and handling) payable to *Silhouette Books*.

Silhouette Books
Book Rack Offer
901 Fuhrmann Blvd.
P.O. Box 1396
Buffalo, NY 14269-1396

*Offer not available in Canada.*

*New York and Iowa residents add appropriate sales tax.

BKR-2A

*Silhouette Special Edition*

NORA ROBERTS'S 50TH SILHOUETTE NOVEL

In May, SILHOUETTE SPECIAL EDITION celebrates Nora Roberts's "golden anniversary"— her 50th Silhouette novel!

*The Last Honest Woman* launches a three-book "family portrait" of entrancing triplet sisters. You'll fall in love with all THE O'HURLEYS!

> *The Last Honest Woman*—May
> Hardworking mother Abigail O'Hurley Rockwell finally meets a man she can trust...but she's forced to deceive him to protect her sons.
>
> *Dance to the Piper*—July
> Broadway hoofer Maddy O'Hurley easily lands a plum role, but it takes some fancy footwork to win the man of her dreams.
>
> *Skin Deep*—September
> Hollywood goddess Chantel O'Hurley remains deliberately icy...until she melts in the arms of the man she'd love to hate.

Look for THE O'HURLEYS! And join the excitement of Silhouette Special Edition!

SSE451-1